"You're a cool o...

"Walking back into my life…*crawling* into my bed just as though the last five years have never happened."

Annie felt as though a huge weight was crushing down inside her.

"Please," she croaked. "I don't understand."

"Do you think I understood when you walked out on me…on our marriage?"

Their *marriage…!*

"We can't be married," she whispered painfully. "I don't know you…."

"Now I have heard everything. Tell me, Annie, do you make a habit of going to bed with men you don't know? Is that another part of your personality I never knew existed? Just like your propensity for disappearing without explanation?"

Twice now he had mentioned her walking out on him…disappearing. What kind of relationship must they have had for her to do that?

"I can't stay here. I have to go," she began unsteadily.

"No way! Not until you've told me why you did it, Annie. Why you walked out on me."

Amnesia

**What the memory has lost,
the body never forgets**

An electric chemistry with
a disturbingly familiar stranger....
A reawakening of passions long forgotten....
And a compulsive desire to get to know this
stranger all over again!

A brand-new miniseries from
Harlequin Presents® featuring top-selling authors:
Penny Jordan, Susan Napier
and **Lynne Graham**

In October, don't miss
Secret Seduction
by
Susan Napier
#2135

Penny Jordan

BACK IN THE MARRIAGE BED

Amnesia

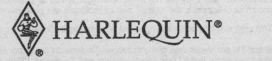

TORONTO • NEW YORK • LONDON
AMSTERDAM • PARIS • SYDNEY • HAMBURG
STOCKHOLM • ATHENS • TOKYO • MILAN • MADRID
PRAGUE • WARSAW • BUDAPEST • AUCKLAND

If you purchased this book without a cover you should be aware
that this book is stolen property. It was reported as "unsold and
destroyed" to the publisher, and neither the author nor the
publisher has received any payment for this "stripped book."

ISBN 0-373-12129-6

BACK IN THE MARRIAGE BED

First North American Publication 2000.

Copyright © 2000 by Penny Jordan.

All rights reserved. Except for use in any review, the reproduction or
utilization of this work in whole or in part in any form by any electronic,
mechanical or other means, now known or hereafter invented, including
xerography, photocopying and recording, or in any information storage
or retrieval system, is forbidden without the written permission of the
publisher, Harlequin Enterprises Limited, 225 Duncan Mill Road,
Don Mills, Ontario, Canada M3B 3K9.

All characters in this book have no existence outside the imagination of
the author and have no relation whatsoever to anyone bearing the same
name or names. They are not even distantly inspired by any individual
known or unknown to the author, and all incidents are pure invention.

This edition published by arrangement with Harlequin Books S.A.

® and TM are trademarks of the publisher. Trademarks indicated with
® are registered in the United States Patent and Trademark Office, the
Canadian Trade Marks Office and in other countries.

Visit us at www.eHarlequin.com

Printed in U.S.A.

CHAPTER ONE

ANNIE paused halfway up the stairs of her pretty Victorian cottage, a softly tantalising smile curling her mouth in secret appreciation, a dreamy, distant look hazing the normal clarity of her widely spaced intelligent grey eyes. She had had the dream again last night, the one that featured 'him'. And *this* time, *last* night, he had been even more deliciously real than ever before. So real, in fact...

As her cheeks pinkened betrayingly and her eyelashes modestly swept down to conceal the expression her eyes might inadvertently betray, Annie could feel the sharp thrill of remembered pleasure running hotly through her body. Last night when he had held her, touched her... A fierce shiver openly tensed her body and a little guiltily she hurried the rest of the way upstairs.

She only had an hour to get ready before leaving to collect Helena and her husband. The three of them were going out for a special celebratory meal, and by rights it was *that* she ought to be thinking about, not some impossibly wonderful and totally unreal man she had created out of her own imagination, her own dreams...her own *need*...

Her frown deepened a little. For a woman of twenty-three without a man in her life, without a *lover* in her life, the sheer intensity of the sensuality of the periodic dreams she had about the fantasy male she had mentally labelled her perfect lover, her soul mate and other half, were becoming increasingly explicit. A sign of her loveless, manless state, or an indication of the power of her imagination? Annie didn't know. What she did know, though, was that since she had first started dreaming about him none of the real men she had met had had the power to compare with him, nor to touch her emotions.

She was looking forward to the evening ahead. Helena was not, after all, just her closest friend and a substitute mother figure to her; she was also the woman, the *surgeon*, who was responsible for saving her life. No, Annie corrected herself quickly, what Helena was responsible for in many ways was *giving* her life, giving it back to her after others, less determined, less compassionate, less seeing, had said that...

Tensely Annie swallowed. Even now, nearly five years after the event, after the accident which had so nearly cost her her life, the mere thought of how close she had come to death had the power to strike an icy chill of terror right through her.

Perhaps illogically, the fact that she had no memory, either of the events leading up to the accident itself nor the weeks when she had been in a coma, made her fear of how easily she might not have survived all the more intense.

As she pushed at her bedroom door the slight awkwardness of her arm, which was the sole physical legacy she now had left of the accident, showed itself in the way she had to open it. Her arm had been so badly crushed, so badly damaged, that the senior registrar on duty when she had been rushed into the accident unit had been on the point of having her prepared for an amputation when Helena, who had only dropped in at the hospital to see another patient, had happened to walk through the unit and had been called over by him for a second opinion.

As the hospital's senior microsurgeon Helena had immediately taken charge, deciding it might be possible to save Annie's arm.

Her face had been the first one Annie had seen when she had first regained consciousness, but it hadn't been for many, many weeks after that that she had learned, not from Helena herself but from one of the nurses, how lucky she was that Helena had chanced to be in the hospital when she had been brought in.

It had been Helena who had spent hour after hour at her bedside talking to her whilst she lay in a coma, dragging her with the strength of her will and her love back to the world of the living, and Annie knew that she would never, never cease to revere and love her for all that she had done.

'You aren't the only one who has gained,' Helena often teased her gently. 'You have no idea how much higher my professional stock has grown since it's become publicly known that my personal surgical procedure saved your arm. Your arm is worth more than its weight in gold to me, Annie...' And then her face would soften as she'd add, far more tenderly, 'And you, my dear, are more special to me than I can find the words to say. The daughter I never thought I would have...'

Both of them had cried a little the first time Helena had made this loving claim, the moment and the words especially meaningful to them both. Helena, the highly qualified and skilled surgeon who had lost her own womb and her chances of motherhood at a very young age, and Annie, the girl who had been abandoned as a baby and then grown up in a children's home, always treated well but never loved in that special one-to-one way she had so often yearned for.

Two years ago, when Helena had finally accepted the proposal of marriage from her long-term partner Bob Lever, Annie had been more pleased for both of them than she had been able to find the words to say.

Previously Helena had always refused to marry Bob, claiming that one day he might meet a woman who could give him the children she couldn't and that when that day came she wanted him to feel free to go to her, and it had taken the combined efforts of both Annie and Bob to persuade her to think differently.

In the end it had been Annie's gentle reminder that since Helena had unofficially adopted her as her 'daughter' she no longer had any reason for refusing Bob's proposals.

'Very well. I give in,' Helena had laughed, waiting until they had finished toasting her acceptance of Bob's proposal before adding, tongue in cheek to Annie, 'Of course, you know what this means, don't you? As your ''mother'', and at my time of life,

Annie, I shall soon be urging you to find yourself a mate and produce some grandchildren for me.'

It had been after that, and relaxed by the excellence of the Christmas dinner she and Helena had cooked together and the wine that had accompanied it, that Annie had been able to tell Helena the extraordinary intensity of the dreams she had been having.

'When did they first start?' Helena had questioned her, immediately very professional.

'I'm not sure... I think I must have been having them for a while before I actually *knew* I was,' Annie had told her, shaking her head and laughing at her own confusing statement.

'You see, when I did start to realise I was having them they seemed so familiar, as though he had been a part of my life for always... It was as though somehow...I...I knew him...' She had stopped speaking to frown and shake her head as she tried to grapple for the right words to describe the extraordinary complexity of the feelings within her dreams, to convey to her friend the reality of the man who featured in them.

Now, though, as she headed for her wardrobe to remove the new dress she and Helena had bought especially for this occasion the previous month, she caught sight of her reflection and gave another small smile. She had been so lucky that her face hadn't been damaged at all in the accident. Small and heart-shaped, it still looked pretty much as it did in the few photographs she had of her childhood. Her hair was still the same blonde colour—an inheritance from her unknown parent, along with the elegance of her bone structure. Maturity, and the much stronger sense of self she had developed, meant that she no longer agonised over who and what her parents had been. It was enough that they had given the most precious gift there was—the gift of life itself.

All she knew of the accident was what she had been told, what had been said during the court case, which had resulted in the driver who had knocked her down on the pedestrian crossing she had been halfway over being convicted of dangerous driving and his insurance company being compelled to make a very large payment to her indeed.

Annie knew there were those who thought enviously that a weakened right arm and being out of action for almost a year were only minor inconveniences to have to put up with. Certainly the driver's insurance company's legal team had thought so, and Annie was the first to agree that because of the accident she had gained enormously—not because of the insurance company pay-out but because it had brought Helena and Bob into her life.

As the lawyers for the insurance company had been quick to point out, her injuries had not prevented her from going on to complete the degree course she had been just about to start when the accident happened, nor had it precluded her from obtaining a job. Indeed, for many people, the fact that she was only able to work part-time at the moment, job-sharing with another girl, would be a plus point and not a minus one.

Oh, yes, the lawyers for the defence had been very, very persuasive, but the evidence had been damning.

There had been five witnesses who had each seen the way the car had been driven across the pedestrian crossing and straight into Annie. The driver had been drinking—a stress-related problem which he now had under control, according to his defence.

Annie sighed. There had even been a tearful appearance by his wife, who'd said that without her husband's income, without his ability to earn a living, if he lost his licence for too long a period, the lives of her and her three small children would be made very hard indeed.

Annie's tender heart had ached for them, and still often did, but, as Helena had told her robustly, *she* was not the one who was responsible for their plight.

Even so, she was glad that the driver of the car had been from out of town and that there was no chance that she was likely to bump into him locally—or his family.

It seemed odd to her now to think that she had not lived the whole of her life here in this small, sleepy cathedral city, with its history, its castle, its small university and its river—the river which had once, many, many years ago, been the major source of its wealth and position. Now, though, the boats that used the pretty marina were strictly pleasure craft; the merchant vessels which had once brought their exotic wares to the port belonged to another era altogether.

Annie couldn't remember just why she had chosen to apply to Wryminster's university for a place, nor when she had arrived in the city. She had clearly not had time to make any friends or to confide her dreams or ambitions to them. The accident had happened just before the week of the new term—her first week, her first term—and the only address the authorities had been able to find on Annie had been that of the children's home where she had grown up.

According to what Helena had been able to find out she had been a quite clever child, and something of a loner. It had been Helena who had taken her home when at last the hospital had discharged her. Helena who had mothered her, cared for her, *loved* her. And Helena, too, who had encouraged her in her need to become properly independent, she and Bob helping Annie to find her perfect little home not too far from their own house.

As she slipped the new outfit she and Helena had bought together from its protective wrapper Annie expelled a small shaky breath. She had come so far to reach this day, had *had* to come so far... The outfit was a soft icy blue, a perfect foil for her skin tone and her eyes. She had fallen in love with it the minute she had seen it, although it had taken a lot of persuasion and coaxing from Helena before she had finally given in and bought it.

In soft fine wool crêpe the trousers showed off the slender length of her legs and the narrow delicacy of her hips whilst the almost full-length coat added a breathtakingly stylish elegance to the ensemble. Beneath the coat there was a pretty embroidered top to add a final touch of glamour.

'I won't get my money's worth out of it,' Annie had predicted, shaking her head as she'd paid for it. 'I don't go anywhere I can wear something so expensive.'

'Well, perhaps you ought to start,' Helena had smiled. 'Sayad would do anything to get you to agree to a date.'

Sayad was a very, very dishy anaesthetist who had recently joined the hospital staff, and he had made a bee line for Annie the moment he had seen her.

'He's nice,' she had responded, quickly shaking her head. 'But...'

But not her dream man. Oh, no—nowhere even near her dream man. Where Sayad was merry and open-faced her dream lover was dark-browed and almost brooding; a *man* where Sayad was still in some ways, despite his age, part boy. Without knowing *how* she knew, she *knew* that her dream lover would have an air of authority and masterfulness, an aura of such strong maleness that Sayad could never in any way really compare with him.

Despite her reservations about the cost of her new outfit, she had given way in the end because tonight was a special celebration: her close friends Bob and Helena's wedding anniversary and Bob's birthday.

At Helena's insistence, following the successful conclusion of the long drawn-out legal battle she had endured before winning substantial damages for her injury, she was taking a few months' sabbatical from her job. Earlier in the week she had said her temporary goodbyes to her colleagues at the multinational petrochemical company, Petrofiche, whose head offices were situated in what had originally been a very large country house several miles outside the city, over a happy girlie lunch.

For this evening's meal she had booked a table at

the area's most prestigious restaurant on the river, insisting that on this occasion *she* was going to treat Helena and Bob, and that she would pick them up in her newly acquired and rather swish Mercedes car.

The car had been a real step forward for Annie. She hadn't been able to drive when she had had her accident, and for a long time afterwards she had remained terrified of even being near a car never mind driving one. But eventually she had forced herself to overcome her fears and she had successfully taken her test. The weakness in her arm meant that she felt much more comfortable driving an automatic car than a manual, and so, aided and abetted by Helena and Bob, she had finally given in and allowed herself the luxury of her new smart car.

It didn't take her long to get ready; she preferred to use the minimum of make-up and, as Helena often told her enviously, she was lucky enough to have naturally good skin. If her mouth was a little too full for her own liking, well, she had learned how to tone down its sizzling second glance male appeal with pastel-toned lipsticks. Her hair, silky and straight, she always wore long and simply styled, setting off her delicate bone structure.

Once on, the new outfit looked even better than Annie had remembered. She had finally, this last year, with the court case at long last behind her, started to put on a little extra weight and it suited her.

Giving her bedroom a proud appraisal, she walked over to the door. Her small Victorian cottage, bought out of the award the court had given her, had been very run-down when she had found it, and she had lived surrounded by builders' rubble and very often the builders themselves whilst it was being restored and renovated, determinedly refusing Helena and Bob's pleas for her to move back in with them until the work was finished. She had wanted to be on the spot, to prove her maturity and her independence and, most of all, to prove to *herself* that she was capable of managing on her own.

The large double bed which dominated the room couldn't help but catch her eye. Even now she wasn't quite sure *why* she had bought it, *why* she had so instinctively and automatically picked it out of all the beds in the showroom, heading for it almost like someone on autopilot, or someone who was sleep-walking.

All she had known was that it was the bed she had to have.

'Well, it will certainly suit the house,' had been Helena's comment when she had taken her to see it, and she had admired its reproduction Victorian styling.

In her dreams she and her dream lover were always in this bed, although in her dreams... Guiltily Annie reminded herself that she was going to be late picking up her friends if she didn't make a move.

Her face slightly more pink than it had been, she headed downstairs.

'Goodness, this place looks busy this evening,' Helena commented as Annie carefully reversed her car into the single parking space left in the restaurant's car park.

'Yes, they did say when I originally booked the table that they were expecting a busy evening. Apparently Petrofiche are having a dinner for their new consultant marine biologist.'

'Oh, yes, I heard they'd found someone to take Professor Salter's place. They've headhunted him from one of the Gulf States, or so I've heard. He's extremely highly qualified and relatively young—in his thirties. It seems he's actually worked for Petrofiche in the past.'

'Mmm… It's odd to think of a marine biologist working for the petrochemical industry,' Bob cut in.

Helena gave him a wifely smile and then exchanged a conspiratorial look with Annie as she teased him,

'I suppose *you* think of marine biologists as people who make underwater films of sharks and coral reefs…'

'No, of course I don't,' Bob denied, but his sheepish look gave him away.

'These days all the large multi-nationals are keen to ensure that their customers see them as greener than green and very environmentally aware,' Annie told them both. 'And because of the effect any kind of oil seepage has on the world's seas and oceans, and their life forms, for companies like Petrofiche it makes good sense to use the services of such experts.'

They were out of the car now and heading towards the restaurant. Originally a private house, it had been very successfully converted to an exclusive restaurant, complete with a conservatory area and a stunningly beautiful garden which ran down to the river. As they walked past the wrought-iron gates that led to the private garden they could see inside it, where skilful lighting illuminated several of the specimen trees as well as the courtyard area and its decorative statues.

The restaurant was owned and run by a husband and wife team in their late thirties, and as she recognised them Liz Rainford gave them a warm, welcoming smile.

'I've kept you your favourite table,' she whispered to them as she signalled to a waiter to take them through to the dining room.

Liz was on the committee of a local charity that Annie helped out, by volunteering for fund raising duties when she could, and Liz was aware of the history of Annie's accident and her relationship with Helena and Bob.

'I know tonight's a special night for all of you.' She smiled.

Their favourite table was one that was tucked quite discreetly in a corner by one of the windows, through which one could see down the length of the garden and beyond it to the river, and as their waiter settled them in their chairs and produced their menus with a theatrical flourish Annie gave a small sigh of pleasure.

Sometimes she felt almost as though she had been reborn on that morning five years ago when she had opened her eyes in her hospital bed to see Helena looking back at her. Although now she could remember her childhood and her teenage years, they were somehow in soft focus and slightly unreal, their edges blurred, so that occasionally it was hard for her to remember that those years, those *memories*, actually did belong to her.

It was the effect of the huge trauma her mind and body had experienced, Helena was quick to say, to comfort her when she worried about it; her mind's way of protecting her.

The restaurant was full, with the doors to the conservatory closed to protect the privacy of the party from Petrofiche dining inside it. The girls in the office had been talking about the new consultant when Annie had been at work earlier in the week.

'He's got his own business and Petrofiche is just *one* of his clients,' Beverley Smith, one of the senior personal assistants, had told them importantly. 'He'll only be coming in here a couple of days a week when he isn't out in the field.'

'Mmm... I wonder if he needs a PA. *I* certainly wouldn't mind a couple of trips to the Barrier Reef,' one of the other girls had remarked enviously.

'The Barrier Reef!' another had scoffed. 'More like Alaska. *That's* the current hot-spot for marine biologists.'

Annie had listened to their good-natured bantering with a small smile.

Although she was regularly invited out on dates by male members of the staff she never accepted. Helena had warned her gently that she was in danger of allowing her dream lover to blind her to the reality of real live potential mates, but Annie was quietly aware that there was more to her reluctance to accept dates than merely a romantic figment of her own idealistic dreams.

It was almost as though, in some way, something deep within her told her that it would be wrong for her to start seeing someone. Quite why she should think this she was at a loss to know, and, indeed, her feelings were so nebulous, so inexplicable, that she felt too foolish to even confide them to Helena. All she did know was that for some reason it was necessary for her to wait…but to wait for what? For whom? She had no idea. She just knew it was something she had to do!

CHAPTER TWO

'OH, WE didn't order champagne,' Annie began as the waiter suddenly appeared with a bottle and three glasses, and then stopped as she saw the look of smiling complicity Helena and Bob were exchanging.

'This was supposed to be *my* treat,' she reproached them as the waiter filled their champagne flutes.

'Yes, I know, but it *is* our celebration,' Bob reminded her fondly.

Annie agreed quietly, her eyes large and dark with the emotional intensity of her thoughts, tears just beginning to film them as she turned to Helena and told her huskily, 'If it hadn't been for you...' She stopped, unable to go on, and the three of them sat in silence as they each shared the others' emotions.

It was Bob who broke the emotional intensity of the moment, picking up his glass and lifting it, announcing in a firm voice, 'To you, Annie...'

'Yes, my love. To you,' Helena joined in the toast.

As she looked at Annie's flushed face Helena marvelled at the recuperative powers of the human body and its capacity for endurance. Looking at Annie, it was hard to equate the healthy young woman she was now with the comatose, badly injured accident victim she had seen lying inert on the hospital trolley as she'd hurried through the Accident and Emergency unit.

Later, whilst they were waiting for their pudding course, Annie excused herself to the other two.

'I'm just going to the loo,' she announced, getting up and walking towards the cloakrooms in the foyer. She was just about to walk past the entrance to the conservatory when the door opened and a party of four men came out. Two of them Annie recognised as executives from the company she worked for, the third she didn't know, and the fourth...

Her heart gave a stunned leap inside her chest wall, shock rooting her to the floor where she stood as she stared open-mouthed at the fourth member of the quartet in total disbelief.

It was him! He... The man... From her dreams... So exactly identical to him that she could only stand and stare in silent shock. Her dream lover come to life! But how could that be possible when he was only a figment of her own imagination, a creature she had conjured up within her own mind? No, it *wasn't* possible. She must be imagining it...hallucinating... She had drunk too much champagne she decided dizzily.

Quickly she closed her eyes and counted to ten, and then she opened them. He was still there, and what was more he was looking at her. She felt as though her blood was quite literally draining from her veins, leaving her empty, her body cold and in danger. Panic filled her. She tried to move and couldn't. She tried to speak but no sound emerged from her paralysed throat... A hideous, horrible sensation of fear invaded her. She *wanted* to move. She *wanted* to speak. But she couldn't. With horrible certainty Annie knew that she was going to faint.

When she came round she was in Liz's private quarters and Bob and Helena were hovering anxiously over her.

'Darling, what is it...what happened?' Helena was asking her worriedly as she chafed her hand. Helen's fingers were on her pulse, Annie recognised shakily, and she could see the professional beginning to take over from the concerned friend. Determinedly she forced herself to sit up.

'I'm all right,' she insisted. 'I just felt faint, that's all,' she whispered, still too much in shock to be able to tell Helena what had actually happened.

'I'm sorry,' she apologised to Liz as she ignored Helena's protests and swung her feet to the floor, gritting her teeth against her giddiness as she made herself stand up. 'I don't really have much of a head for vintage champagne,' she excused herself, giving the other woman a brief smile.

Of course there was no question of either Helena or Bob allowing her to drive home, nor of her being allowed to return home on her own. Instead she was put to bed in the bedroom which had been hers whilst she was recuperating, with Helena fussing round her and announcing that she felt it might be a good idea if she were to have a full check-up.

'There's nothing wrong with me,' Annie insisted. 'I just had a bit of a shock, that's all.'

'A shock? What kind of shock?' Helena demanded anxiously.

'I...I thought I saw someone I...' Annie paused

and shook her head, her mouth dry as she told her, 'I must have made a mistake, imagined it. I know, because it just isn't possible that...'

'Who was it? *Who* did you think you saw, Annie?' Helena probed.

'It...it wasn't anyone. It was...just...just a mistake,' Annie repeated stubbornly, but as she reached for the cup of tea Bob had brought her she started to tremble so violently that she had to put it down again.

Covering her face with her hands she admitted shakily, 'Oh, Helena...it was so...so surreal. I don't...I saw *him*...the man...from my dreams... He was...' She stopped and shook her head. 'I *know* that I *can't* have done, that he just doesn't exist, but...'

'You're getting yourself all worked up,' Helena told her firmly. 'I'll give you something to help you relax and go to sleep, and then in the morning we can talk about it properly.'

As she lay back against the pillows Annie gave her a small weak smile. She knew that her friend was right, of course.

Several minutes later Helena, who had left the room, came back with a glass of water and two tablets for her to take. She watched with maternal tenderness as Annie dutifully swallowed them down.

'I'm sorry if I spoiled your evening,' she whispered drowsily to Helena as the tablets started to work.

Now that she was beginning to feel calmer she couldn't understand why she had overreacted so foolishly, just because of some minor and no doubt imagined similarity between the man she had seen in the restaurant and her own fantasy lover. And anyway, now that she *really* thought about it, there was no way her dream lover would *ever* have looked at her the way the man in the restaurant had, with that look of implacable cold hostility in his dense, darkly blue eyes, that blanked-out look of icy contempt and banked-down anger.

Wearily Annie felt her eyes starting to close, and ten minutes later, when Helena quietly shut the bedroom door behind herself, Annie was deeply and completely asleep.

'I suspect that the emotion of the evening and the memories it stirred up are the root cause of what happened,' Helena announced to her husband Bob as she went back downstairs to join him.

'Mmm… There's no way the man she saw *could* be someone she knew, is there?' Bob asked her curiously.

'Well, it *is* a possibility I suppose,' Helena agreed. 'After all, as you know, there are still some missing pieces from her memory. She can remember arriving here in Wryminster, but she *can't* remember *when* she arrived. It's difficult to imagine that anyone who was involved with her to the extent they would *have had* to be involved with her to be responsible for dreams of the intensity of those that Annie has been having could ever be cold-hearted enough, uncaring enough, not to get in touch after the accident. After all, it was reported in the local papers.'

'No, it does seem improbable,' Bob agreed.

*   *   *

Upstairs in her sleep Annie started to smile, her body quivering with a mixture of nervousness and excitement.

'God, but you feel so good… Will you let me look at you as well as hold you, little Annie? I want to so much…'

Annie tensed a little as the warm, knowing male hands began to gently undress her, nervous at first, her heart thumping anxiously, but then, as pleasure and excitement took over from her initial apprehension, her tension started to fade, her body beginning to relax as she started to respond to the soft verbal praise of her lover whilst he, oh, so slowly and carefully, laid her body bare to his gaze, peeling back the protective layers of her clothing, freeing her flesh to the warmth of his hands, their warmth, like their strength, a benediction as well as a nerve-thrilling wonderful new sensation.

He knew that this was her first real experience of a man's love, her first time, and he had told her, reassured her, that the choice, the decision was to be hers, that he would, if she asked him to do so, stop and allow her to change her mind. But she didn't *want* to change her mind, nor did she want him to *stop*. She wanted…

She gave a small gasp of delight as his touch set fire to her desires, igniting all the passion she had somehow known she was capable of feeling but which hitherto had been locked up inside her, hidden away in a secret place to which only he had the key.

She loved him so much…wanted him so much… What had been unthinkable with anyone else was not just 'thinkable' with him, but desirable…must-haveable… Her whole body shook with the force of what she was feeling…with her longing for him…her love for him. He only had to look at her and she melted.

Just the way he said her name was a form of poetry greater than even the greatest love sonnets. Just the way he looked at her more beautiful than any love song ever sung. The way he made her feel was so intense it was scary… He thrilled her, excited her, made her want to laugh and cry at the same time, filled her with such happiness that it made her feel afraid. *He* made her feel almost immortal, and yet, at the same time, he filled her with such a sense of her fragile vulnerability, her own frightening dependence on him and his love, that she was consumed with terror at the thought of losing him.

He stroked her breasts, watching her as she quivered in instant response, her eyes darkening, her lips parting.

'Has anyone ever told you that you have the sexiest mouth in the whole world?' he asked her softly, rimming it with his fingertip and smiling as she made an instinctive movement to catch hold of it.

'Not like that,' he whispered to her. 'Like this…' And then he slid his fingertip into her mouth, coaxing her to fasten her lips around it and slowly suck on it.

In her dream Annie moaned out loud in shocked delight, her body moving restlessly as it sought the intimacy of its lover's embrace.

The evening sun slanted through the wide windows. Beyond them, if she opened her eyes, Annie knew she would see the purple haze of the distant hills, and if she stood close to them she could look down on the mellow wash of the river. Even at this distance she could hear its soft rhythmic whisper, almost feel the insidious pull of its tide, just as she could feel the urgent tug of the female tide within her own body. She drew a sharp breath as she felt the male hunger in the hands that caressed her.

'Tell me now if you want me to stop,' he was whispering huskily, *insistently*, to her. 'Tell me now, Annie, otherwise it will be too late.'

But she knew she would say nothing, that she wanted him too much, loved him too much, even though the things he was doing to her, *with* her, were a world away from her own childish experience, limited to a few fumbled kisses.

'I'm much, much too old for you,' he had already told her, but somehow, instead of putting her off, his bold confession had only heightened and intensified her desire for him, imbuing him with a magical, almost mystical worldliness, a male knowledge and awareness that galvanised her body into excited little shivers.

And now it was nearly here, the moment of supreme revelation, the moment when...

Annie gave a sharp, piercing cry and she suddenly woke up, her body drenched in perspiration, her mind racing. As she sat up in her bed she covered her face with trembling hands.

Her dream had been so strong, so real, and the

man in it, her dream lover, had been so—so scarily alive.

Shakily she tried to draw a calming breath of air into her lungs, and then she closed her eyes, reliving the moment when she had traced with her lips the shape of the tiny scar she had seen on her lover's temple, the same scar in exactly the same spot that the man in the restaurant had had. How many times had she dreamed of that scar and not really known it?

She didn't know. She only knew that a small fierce stillness had gripped him as she touched it. It was as familiar to her as her own reflection. But how could that be? What was happening to her? Was she experiencing some kind of sixth sense, some kind of special awareness, some kind of inexplicable glimpse into the future? Were they perhaps fated to meet, and was this—these dreams—fate's way of warning her of what was to come, of what was to be? Her whole body started to tremble.

She had been so very close to death, and, although she was extremely loath to acknowledge it, never mind discuss it openly, had experienced the sensation she had read avidly and secretly about that was reportedly so common to people who shared her near-death experience: that feeling of rushing towards a wonderful welcoming place, being propelled through darkness into an indescribable sense of awesome light, then that sudden awareness of being turned back, pulled back, that voice that was not actually a voice announcing that it was not yet her time.

Had that experience somehow or other, illogical

and implausible though it might sound, given her the ability to sense, to feel, to experience a special, wonderful event in her life that had yet to take place?

Had the secret yearning she had carried all her life, to share it with someone who loved her, affected her to such an extent that she was already living in her dreams what she had yet to live in reality? Was her dream lover, in fact, not so much a figment of her imagination as a very factual and real figure from her future?

Impossible, implausible... Yes, maybe, but then there were many mysterics that defied logical explanation and analysis.

The fear she had felt earlier in the evening, the sense of shock and panic, had given way to an excitement that was almost euphoric. Her dream lover wasn't just a dream. He was real. He was... Ecstatically Annie closed her eyes, hugging her thoughts, her love, to her heart just as tightly as she yearned for him to hug and hold her.

It was a long time before she finally got back to sleep, and when she did finally succumb her exalted state had convinced her that the evening's meeting with the real-life physical embodiment of her dream man had been an act of fate for which her dreams had been preparing her.

'Annie, how are you feeling this morning, my love?'

A little groggily Annie focused on Helena as she walked into the bedroom carrying a fragrant mug of coffee.

'I'm not sure,' Annie admitted. 'Those pills you gave me really knocked me out.

'Helena,' she demanded, her voice changing as she sat up in her bed and looked at her friend and mentor with fixed determination. 'Helena, do you believe in…fate?' she asked solemnly.

'I'm not sure just what you mean,' Helena responded cautiously.

'The man—the one I saw in the restaurant last night,' Annie told her in a low voice. 'At first I thought I must be imagining it, that he couldn't possibly be the same man I've been dreaming about… But then, last night, I dreamed about him again, and I knew…'

She took a deep breath and told Helena huskily, 'I think that we must have been destined to meet somehow, Helena, and that he and I…' She paused and shook her head, responding to her friend's silence with a wry, 'Oh, I know how far-fetched this must sound, but what *other* explanation can there be? I don't pretend to know why I should have dreamed about him or why I should feel as though I already know him. I just do. Please don't tell me that you think I'm being silly,' she pleaded.

'I won't,' Helena promised her quietly, pausing to sit on the bed and stroke the soft tumbled hair back off Annie's face with one hand as she placed the mug of coffee on the bedside table with the other.

Annie was so very dear to her, very precious, so much the daughter, the child she herself had never had, but she was also, in Helena's opinion, a very vulnerable young woman. The gravity of her accident and her injuries had meant that the energy that other young women of her age would naturally give to the process of maturing had in Annie's case had to be given to her physical recovery, recuperating her health.

It wasn't that Annie in any way lacked intelligence—far from it. She had obtained her degree and she had a concern for the world and the people in it which made her, in many ways, older and wiser than her peers. But it was a fact that because of the length of time she had spent recovering from the accident Annie had not had the opportunity to mature as a *woman*, to experiment sexually, to make mistakes, errors of judgement, to indulge in all the youthful follies that people normally did on their journey through the turbulent years that led from one's late teens to one's mid-twenties.

Now it seemed that she preferred the fantasy of her dream lover rather than dating a real live man, that she was stubbornly determined to believe in fate rather than reality.

'You *do* think I'm being silly, don't you?' Annie accused Helena flatly as she saw the hesitation in her friend's eyes.

'Not silly,' Helena corrected quietly. 'But perhaps…' She stopped speaking, and then smiled ruefully at Annie before asking her gently, 'Has it occurred to you that this man may have been so familiar to you simply because he *is* familiar?'

'From my dreams, you mean?' Annie checked, nonplussed.

'No. Not from your dreams,' Helena stopped, and

then said quietly, 'Annie, he may have been familiar to you because you do actually know him.'

'*Know* him?' Annie looked perplexed. 'No, that's impossible.'

Helena waited before reminding her softly, 'There *are* still some gaps in your memory, my dear. The weeks leading up to the accident as well as the event itself, and those weeks after, when you were in a coma.'

'Yes, I know.' Annie's forehead creased in a small frown of distress. 'But I couldn't have known him...not the way I feel about him...the way we are... If I had he would have...' She stopped, shaking her head. 'No. It isn't possible,' she told Helena immediately and positively. 'I would have known if he... If I... If we... No,' she reaffirmed.

'Well, I must admit it *does* seem unlikely,' Helena acknowledged slowly. 'But I felt I ought to mention the possibility to you.'

'I understand,' Annie assured her, giving her a warm hug. 'But if he had known me he would have come forward when you advertised, wouldn't he? And besides...' A small secret smile curled her mouth, her eyes suddenly glowing with private happiness. 'I know that if he...if we...' She stopped and shook her head again. 'No. I would have known,' she told Helena calmly. 'I'm sorry I gave you such a shock by fainting like that last night,' she added more prosaically. 'I think it must have been the effect of seeing him so unexpectedly on top of the champagne.'

'Well, it *was* a very emotional evening,' Helena responded.

'You've been so good to me,' Annie told her, lovingly reaching out to cover the older woman's hands with her own.

'Everything I've given to you you've given me back a thousandfold, Annie,' Helena told her lovingly. 'And you are going to give Bob and me our grandchildren,' Helena teased her, deliberately lightening the atmosphere before giving a small exclamation. 'Heavens! Bob! I promised I'd help him with our packing for this conference we're flying out to attend tomorrow. Never mind,' she added with a naughty grin. 'He's so much better at it than I am!'

Annie laughed. 'Four days in Rio de Janeiro... How wonderful.'

'Not as wonderful as you'd think,' Helena countered ruefully. 'The conference goes on for three days, and when you've taken time out for recovering from jet lag and for being dragged all over the place by Bob to see the local ruins...'

'Stop complaining,' Annie teased. 'You know you love it. When the three of us went to Rome last year *I* was the one who had to go back to the hotel for a rest!'

'Yes, that was wonderful, wasn't it?' Helena agreed, getting up off the bed as she told Annie tenderly, 'Don't rush to get up. You might *feel* fine but your body's still in shock.'

'It was just a faint, Helena, that's all,' Annie assured her friend, but she wasn't totally surprised when, later in the day, Helena insisted on driving her to the hospital so that she could be checked over.

'Mothers!' the junior house doctor wisecracked after he had given Annie the all-clear. 'They do love to fuss.'

'Don't they just?' Annie said with a grin, then blushed a little at the admiring looks the young man was giving her.

CHAPTER THREE

'Now, you're sure you're feeling all right?' Helena checked as Annie dropped her and Bob off at the airport.

'I'm fine. Stop fussing,' Annie told her with a good-natured smile as she hugged them both and kissed them goodbye. 'And to prove it I'm going to go home and make a start on that gardening I've been threatening to do for months.'

The garden of her small house was long and narrow, and enclosed at the back by a high brick wall which ensured her privacy but gave the garden a rather closed-in feel.

For Christmas, amongst the other gifts they had given her, Bob and Helena had given her a gardening book with some wonderful ideas plus a very generous gift voucher for a local garden centre, and Annie, who had been studying the book intently, had now come up with her own design for the garden based on the principles in the book.

The first thing she needed, she had decided, was some pretty coloured trellising to place against the walls, and so, after she had watched Bob and Helena's plane take off, she headed back to her car and drove towards the garden centre.

Several happy and productive hours later Annie climbed back into her car again. She had chosen and ordered her trellising, and made arrangements for it to be delivered, as well as getting from the man in charge of the fencing department the telephone number of someone who would come out and fix it in place for her.

As she started her car engine Annie was humming happily to herself. It was a bright sunny day, a brisk breeze sending fluffy white clouds scudding across the sky, and on impulse, instead of taking the direct route back to her own home, Annie opted instead to head towards the river.

The prettily wooded countryside on the outskirts of the town was criss-crossed with narrow country lanes, confusingly so at times—especially when one descended down through the trees and lost sight of the river, as she had just done, Annie recognised as she came to an unmarked fork in the road and paused, not quite sure which road to take.

Instinctively she wanted to take the right-hand fork, even though logic told her the left must lead down towards the river. With a small mental shrug Annie gave in to instinct and then wondered just what she had done as the road she had chosen narrowed virtually to a single track, winding up a sharp steep hillside banked with hedges so thick and high it was impossible for her to gauge just where she was. And yet even though she knew she had never driven up it before Annie felt that the road was somehow familiar.

She gave a small gasp as she rounded a particularly sharp bend and saw in front of her the entrance to a large Victorian house. On the top of each brick gatepost was an odd metal sculpture. The sculptures were made from the harpoons used on the ships of the man who had built this house from the money he had made from his whaling fleet. And *how* had she known *that*? Annie wondered in bemusement as she stopped her car just inside the drive to the house and switched off the engine. She must have read it somewhere, she acknowledged. She had read avidly in the long months of her recovery, books on every subject under the sun, including some on the local history of the area.

And yet... Unsteadily she got out of her car, her heart starting to beat very fast as she walked towards the house. The rhododendrons flanking the drive obscured the sunlight, throwing out dark shadows so that when she actually stepped back into its full beam it dazzled and dizzied her, making her rock slightly on her feet and close her eyes, only to open them again as she felt something coming between her and the warmth of the sun.

'You!' she whispered, her whole body shivering in a mixture of shock and delight as she saw who was standing in front of her. 'It's you,' she whispered a second time, her eyes glowing with bemusement and happiness as she stepped towards the man who had come out of the house to stand in front of her.

Close to and in the daylight he was so exactly the man from her dreams that the awesome nature of the impulse that had brought her here to him held Annie motionless in an invisible bubble of iridescent joy.

It was true. She had been right. There *was* something fateful, fated about him...about them...

Her eyes focused on him, eagerly absorbing every detail of him and mentally checking them off against her own private blueprint. His eyes were exactly the same dark dramatic blue she had dreamed of, his skin the same taut sheeny tan, his hair the same inky almost blue-black. Everything about him was just as she had dreamed—*everything*. Even his mouth. Especially his mouth!

His *mouth*. Annie shivered in sensual delight as she looked at the hard male curve of his upper lip, the sensual promise of his much fuller lower one. If she closed her eyes she would be able to recreate the sensation of it closing over her own, hungrily coaxing her lips to part whilst he caressed them, filling her with his life's breath whilst she...

'So you came.'

His voice reverberated through her, its tone unexpectedly harsh, even a little terse, but wholly recognisable and familiar.

The intensity of her emotions made her shudder as violent spasms of recognition racked her. She had travelled such a long way to reach this moment, this heartbeat out of infinity.

'Yes,' she whispered in response, her voice cracking against the dryness of her throat. 'You...you knew that I would?' she asked, her emotions so heightened that she felt as though she had suddenly entered an extra dimension of awareness.

Behind him she could see the open door to the house. Beyond it, she knew, lay a large hallway, with a table on which would be a bronze of the man who had originally commissioned the house, and into the stairway that curled upwards from it would be carved all manner of sea creatures, both real and mythical; leaping dolphins, graceful whales, octopuses, sea horses and mermaids.

'I...' His voice sounded terse and strained, as though he too was aware of the enormity of what was happening, and as she looked at him and saw the way his gaze suddenly shifted, as though he couldn't quite meet her eyes, she was overwhelmed by a sudden flood of fiercely protective love.

Instinctively she moved towards him, her hand resting lightly on his arm as she whispered protectively, 'It's all right...everything's all right. I'm here. We're...'

Beneath her fingertips she could feel his muscles bunching, clenching, and as she looked up into his face she could see the tight white line of his mouth. Her own body registered the aftershock of what he was feeling in the rush of almost seismic shudders that jolted his body.

'Can we...can we go inside?' she asked him hesitantly.

The house drew her, compelling her to walk towards it. It was almost as though she knew it already, its shape, its rooms, its history, even its scent... Just as she knew *him*...

Now it was her turn to shudder and to tense, but she was already inside the hallway and he was right behind her, blocking out the light from the doorway.

'I never thought this could happen,' she told him simply as she let her dreamy-eyed gaze absorb the wonderful reality of him.

He was tall, much taller than her, but she had known that, and broad too. She already knew just how he would feel and look beneath that soft checked workshirt he was wearing, without those old faded jeans that hugged the taut strength of his thighs. There would be a small scar just inside the right thigh, a tiny indentation, the relic of a boyhood accident. She would place her lips to it and he...

She was trembling wildly now, unable to stop what she was feeling, what she was wanting. A shudder of almost orgasmic sensitivity ripped through her as she watched him. She loved him so much!

'Can we...can we go upstairs?' she asked him huskily, her eyes never leaving his face as she waited for his response.

It seemed a lifetime, an aeon before he replied, both his mouth and his voice oddly stiff as he eventually responded, 'If that's what you want.'

'Yes,' she told him boldly. 'Yes, it is...what I want.' *I want...I want you. I love you.* She ached to tell him, but events were moving too fast to give her time to make such an emotional statement.

Instead...

She started to release his arm and turn towards the stairs, and then, impetuously, she reached up and touched his face with her fingertips, absorbing through them the longed for human warmth, the human reality of his skin, not a dream lover's flesh any more but that of a real man, a real lover.

Although he was clean shaven she could feel the rasp of his skin where he shaved, a prickle of such intense maleness against the acute female sensitivity of her own fingertips that she almost cried out in the raw shock of it, snatching her fingers away as though they had been burned, her eyes wide and dark, almost haunted as she looked up to his.

'You want me,' he said rawly. But it was a statement rather than a question. Still Annie nodded her head, mute, dumb, now that the final moment, the final acknowledgement of what lay between them, of what fate had ordained for them, was actually here.

Her glance darted over his face as nervous as that of a woodland fawn. His eyes…navy blue now, and smouldering with heat; his cheekbones…taut and hard where the flesh stretched across them, his mouth…

She felt giddy, dizzy with the force of her own longing. The silence, the tension between them stretched out like the thinnest of ice over the deepest, coldest and most dangerous water there could be, inviting only the most reckless, only the most foolhardy, to dare its danger.

'Come here,' he commanded her with soft force.

Immediately she did so, closing the gap between them as she moved, almost swayed into the burning inferno of his body heat, the breath driven out of her lungs in a soft, yearning gasp of delirious pleasure as his arms finally closed around her and she turned her face up to his for his kiss, her own lips so soft, swollen, parting with moist longing.

'Oh, yes… Yes… You want me…'

She heard him etch out the sharp, stingingly sensuous words against her mouth, his voice creamy with satisfaction and male pride as his arms made a tight, imprisoning band around her and he bent her back over them, so that the cradle of her pelvis was thrust up tight against his own body.

And then his mouth finally came down on hers in a kiss that her shocked senses registered as being so raw and branding, so determined to imprint on her his stamp of possession, so intent on taking her and breaking her in the most primitive of man to woman embraces that she almost sobbed aloud in an appeal for his awareness of her vulnerability, her lack of experience, her unknowingness. And yet in some confusing way she *did* know, did recognise.

'Was that good?' she heard him asking her in a low, satisfied voice when he finally released her kiss-bitten mouth, and then, before she could answer, before she could move, he was lowering his head again, to make the same hot, mouth-biting love assault on the erect peak of her nipple, his fingers expertly pushing her clothes out of the way of one soft sweetly pink-apexed breast whilst his lips, too hungry to wait, eagerly caressed the other through the thin fabric of her bra and shirt.

For a moment Annie felt almost as though she was going to die from the shock of pleasure that sheeted through her, its intensity such that it made her catch her breath and feel as though her life itself was momentarily held in suspension. Behind her closed eyelids she could see the same brilliant whiteness she remembered from her moment of near-death: pure, burning, intense, soul-touching...like the very best kind of love itself.

Quickly she opened her eyes and focused on his

downbent raven-dark head. The warm flesh of his
exposed nape was a tantalising contradiction of his
stance towards her and her reaction back to him, that
of a man to a woman at its most sensually intense.
That exposed nape was so very much that of a vulnerable boy, a child...the child they would one day
have...

Immediately Annie tensed, as though somehow
something had touched an exposed raw nerve within
her memory. The pain, initially so intense that it had
shocked her into protective immobility, was fading
now, but it still had the power to frighten her.

'What is it? Not second thoughts?' he was asking
her almost brusquely as his lips relinquished possession of her nipple and he lifted his head to look in
her eyes.

In his own there was something, an expression, a
darkness, that made her look away from him.
Somewhere deep within her a pain, a *wariness* was
stirring, but she quickly suppressed it. Nothing...
nothing...could be allowed to spoil this special *magical* coming together. Nothing!

'I...' she began slowly, wanting to find the words
to tell him how she was feeling, to ask him to help
her smother the sharp needle of pain she could feel
threatening her, to disarm it of its potential harm.

But instead of listening to her he shook his head
and said smoothly, 'I thought you wanted us to go
to bed. You *do* want that, don't you, Annie?'

Annie! He knew her *name*. Her heart slammed
fiercely against her ribs, her whole body convulsed
by the sweetly searing surge of her shock.

'I...I want us to make love...' she managed to tell him shakily, before adding breathlessly, so that he would know that her intuition, her knowingness, her acknowledgement of their shared fate matched his, 'Upstairs...in the room...the room...'

'I know which one,' he assured her, and if her ears thought they had caught a rough, searing note of anger beneath the sensual smoothness of his low-toned voice she quickly assured herself that she had to have imagined it.

They walked upstairs together, one step at a time, her body pressed close to his, his arm around her as she leaned helplessly into him. On the half-landing she stopped, automatically gazing through the window towards the river.

'This house was built by a whaling captain,' she told him huskily.

'Yes, I know,' he agreed tersely, his arm dropping momentarily away from her.

'I...I dream about it sometimes,' she told him, searching carefully for the right words to tell him what she had experienced. 'About...the room... and...and about you...'

Without saying anything else she moved back into the protection of his body, only realising that she had been holding her breath a little nervously when his arm finally rose and held her.

They had reached the top of the stairs and were standing in the doorway to the room before he said the words that made her heart turn somersaults of joy inside her body.

'I dream of you too.'

He dreamed of *her*. She *wasn't* alone in her belief…her recognition. Flooded with joy, she turned to him, holding his arm with her hand as she demanded, 'You recognised me, then, the other night…in the restaurant?'

The abrupt, almost reluctant inclination of his head he gave in assent made her ache with female protectiveness. He felt embarrassed, almost afraid to reveal his vulnerability to her. Oh, how much she loved him. How wonderful it was that they had found one another.

'It's going to be so good,' she told him tenderly. '*We* are going to be so good…'

Inside the room everything was just as she had dreamed. The large windows with the view of the drop down to the river and the fields and hills on the other side of it. The floor, wooden, polished, bare. The walls, bare too; the windows with their filmy ethereal curtaining. The bed…

Annie shivered as she saw it, unable to take her gaze off it as her eyes widened and focused unblinkingly on the oh, so familiar iron bedstead. Unlike hers, this, she knew immediately, was original. Very slowly and gently she reached out and touched the frame at the foot of the bed. The metal felt warm to her touch, warm and worn slightly with age. The bed was bigger than hers, much bigger, and piled high with creamy white traditional linen bedding. As she reached down and smoothed the edge of one of the covers she could almost smell the scent of lavender being released by her touch.

'This bed…' she began, dry-mouthed.

'It's a marriage bed,' he told her quickly, and she could almost taste the bitterness in his voice. But before she could question it, turning to him, her eyes quickening with surprise, he was reaching for her, the fierceness, the immediacy of his desire surprising her. She had expected passion, intensity, and even male possessiveness, but this fierce, heated *now*ness he was exhibiting, this silent, hungry concentrated way in which he was reaching for her, holding her...

'Open your mouth. Kiss me properly. You know how,' she could hear him insisting rawly as the fierce, biting intensity of his own kisses threatened to bruise the already swollen softness of her own mouth.

But willingly she complied, wanting only the pleasure she knew she would have in pleasing him. Her breath was drawn into his mouth, mingling with his in a small sobbing moan of acquiescence as he started to imitate the hot, pulsing tide she could feel within her own body, and within his, with small, pulsating thrusts of his tongue. Somehow they were undressing, her own fingers revealing a dexterity, a knowledge she hadn't guessed they possessed.

There was nothing for her to fear, of course. From her dreams she already knew him as he knew her. In them there was not a curve, a corner of one another's bodies they had not explored and enjoyed.

Even so... A fine shudder of female nervousness and shyness ran through her. The merest delicate frisson of sensation, but she knew he could feel it, knew that it was transmitting itself to him where his fingertips touched her flesh.

'You're afraid…'

He made it sound almost as though the thought of her fear pleased him, and Annie's tension increased.

'No,' she denied, her body and her eyes suddenly softening as she told him lovingly, 'How could I ever be afraid…with you?'

It was as though somehow she had unleashed a catalyst, a power, a primitive force that was beyond the control of either of them, because suddenly he had picked her up and was carrying her to the bed, kneeling over her as he laid her down on it, his eyes hot and dark, the colour and heat of a tropical night sky, the flesh of his face drawn so tightly over his bones that she felt compelled to reach out and touch it…him…

A primal sound, a groan, a warning growl, a low, mating purr—Annie did not know which—rasped deep in his throat as he turned his mouth to her hand, nibbling at the tender flesh on the mound of Venus beneath the base of her thumb.

Quivers of hot cataclysmic pleasure melted through her.

'Yes… Yes… Oh, yes,' she heard herself moaning as he continued to undress her, her body arching, moving to accommodate the increasing speed of his hands as the hot ache deep within her flesh manifested itself in a series of revealing uncoordinated jerky movements when she tried to get closer and closer to him. If she closed her eyes she could feel his heat, sense his need. Deep within her mind she already knew his possession, knew the hot, silken sheathed reality of him, the taut, urgent thrust of his body within her own.

A quiver, an ache, a wild yearning need possessed her.

'I want you. I want you,' she told him recklessly over and over again as her own eager fingers tore buttons from their buttonholes, eagerly pushing away the too intrusive fabric of his clothes where they came between them.

In the enclosed cocoon of the bed under the gradual darkening of the evening sky beyond the window she could smell his scent, her nostrils dilating as she deliberately nuzzled closer to him, wanting to absorb more of it…of him…

His chest, where his shirt had fallen open to reveal it, was tanned and taut with muscles, its hard male planes softened with a silky shimmering of fine body hair, so fine, so male, so *him* that it made her fingertips quiver just to touch it, to touch him. She could feel his muscles contracting beneath his skin where she touched him, and her hands spread out in fascinated female delight to span the power of his chest in response to the mute invitation he was giving her. His nipples, dark hard nubs of flesh, puckered into hot hard points of arousal when she touched them, and on a sudden wanton impulse she touched her fingers to her own lips and then to his body, circling each nipple deliberately with her moist fingertips and watching the way his body jerked in fierce quick spasms of reaction.

'Annie stop—you don't know what you're doing to me…' he began, and then groaned. And although

Annie heard the words, and registered the male pride and desire they carried, she was too lost in the pleasure of what she was doing to heed them.

If she were to touch him with her mouth where she had just touched him with her fingers would he...? She bent her head towards him and gasped in shock as he suddenly manacled her wrists with his own hands, pushing her down against the bed whilst he leaned over her.

His jeans, the jeans *she* had unfastened, had moved lower on his hips, revealing the immaculate white flash of his underwear and with it the visibly open evidence of his desire for her.

Annie found that her mouth had suddenly gone very dry and that her body was tensing, aching...wanting. The tremors of need shuddering through her were so intense that she knew he must see them as plainly as she could see him, see them, know them, take pleasure in them...as she was doing in all the signs there were of his arousal and response to her.

Even in her dreams it hadn't been like this, hadn't had this intensity, this needing, this knowing, this immediacy, and she knew without knowing how she knew that her dreams had only been a pale shadow of what would be reality.

'You want me,' he repeated, and as she smiled at him Annie suddenly felt so powerful, so womanly, so desirous and desirable, that when he released her hands it was the most natural, the most beautiful act in the world for her to stand up, reach out and tug down his jeans, her gaze lifting to his, meshing with his as her hands slid over his thighs towards the white glimmer of fabric that kept him hidden from her.

And then, when just for a heartbeat she hesitated, she heard him growling fiercely, 'Do it... Do it...'

His words were both a command and a plea, and a teasing female smile curled Annie's mouth as she moved to obey them. But it was a smile that died away, wiped out by the rolling flood of emotions that stormed her when she finally saw him naked.

Dreams were...just dreams. And *this* was...*he* was...reality. A small, sharp sob escaped her as mingled pain and pleasure arced through her, and without thinking what she was doing she made to wrap her arms around him, to rest her face against him, the tears of emotion that were clouding her eyes spilling over onto his skin.

'No.' The sharp rejection in his voice shocked and bewildered her as he started to thrust her away.

But the look on his face as she looked enquiringly towards him, searching his expression for an explanation of his rejection, locked her own breath in her throat and made her heart hammer so furiously with reciprocal emotion that she couldn't even begin to articulate what she wanted to say.

She forgot the tight grip of his hands on her arms, forgot too the initial thrust of rejection and shock she had felt when he had first given that harsh cry of denial. In a face that was bleached of all its colour his eyes glittered with such a look of raw torment that Annie couldn't drag her gaze away from them.

It was, she recognised, like looking into his soul

and seeing laid bare there all of man's strongest and most self-weakening emotions. Pain, anguish, anger, longing, need. She could see them all, and as she witnessed his vulnerability Annie felt her heart melt with love and tenderness towards him.

Why he should be exhibiting such strong and in so many ways contradictory emotions she had no idea. What she did know, though, was that he needed her comfort and her compassion, and automatically she reached out to him, wanting to give them to him, wanting to wrap him protectively in her love, to soothe and reassure him.

Emotional tears of protective love filled her eyes as Annie stood body to body with him.

'I love you,' she told him softly. 'I've always loved you and I always will.'

Something flashed in his eyes, an emotion, a response so brief and intense that it was gone before Annie could seize on it to recognise it, but she could hear the fury in his voice as he stepped back from her, demanding savagely, 'How can you say that?'

He was angry…questioning her love. Why, when he must know as deeply as she did, that…?

'You don't want me?' she questioned him shakily, her mouth starting to tremble and her face colouring. He gave a brief look at his own self-betraying body before telling her with raw sensuality, 'Does it look like I don't? Of course I damned well *want* you,' he told her savagely. 'And you want me too, don't you, Annie? Oh, yes, you want me.' He answered his own question, his voice as thick and soft as cream as he took control of the situation from her, reaching for her and drawing her into his arms, his kiss so delicate and tender, so tantalising and erotic that beneath her breath Annie gave a small moan of female longing, instinctively pressing her body as close to his as she could get it, revelling in the hot, silken naked feeling of his flesh against her own, shivering, shuddering as she responded helplessly to her own need for him.

Just to be with him like this, to be free to see, smell, touch the reality of him, not just dream about him.

Her feelings threatened to overwhelm her with such a flood of wanting that she had to close her eyes, her body suddenly so weak, powerless to resist the eroticism of her own thoughts.

'Oh, yes, you want me,' she heard him saying thickly to her with soft male satisfaction as he licked and nuzzled her skin. 'You want me and you're going to have me, Annie. All of me...all of me whilst *I* take all of you...'

It was everything she had dreamed of and more. A hot, silken, perfect meshing of limbs and mouths and then ultimately of the very essence of their two selves.

She had dreamed so often of this intimacy, had thought she had known all there was to know of it, and in many ways she did—in many ways she knew him so well already that her body was perfectly prepared for him, perfectly ready and eager. But in others...

A soft moan of pleasure escaped her lips as she looked down at their entwined bodies through half-closed eyes to watch as he moved up, over her and then within her quickly, but not before a staccato of gasps of shocked ecstasy as she saw how big he was, how perfectly he filled her, saw how wonderful...how good...how meant to be they looked together. And then she was past thinking, past observing, past *anything* other than simply being, responding, loving.

Adoringly Annie raised her face towards his, her lips parting for his kiss, her hands reaching out to draw him closer as he seemed to hesitate. Each thrust of his body within her own took her, drove her towards the wonderful rainbow-coloured place that was just so tantalisingly out of reach. And then suddenly it was there, and she was a part of it, transmuted by love and passion into a quicksilver explosion of heat and pleasure as he took her through the rainbow to a place beyond it, a sphere, a universe, a love-produced paradise of pleasure she had never, ever imagined existed.

As the final echoes of her orgasm slowly faded away Annie stretched luxuriously, so dizzy with happiness that it was impossible for her to find the words to say how she felt. Instead she simply reached out and lovingly touched his face with her fingertips, her eyes huge and dark with emotion, her mouth trembling.

'I love you so much,' she told him chokily. 'I hadn't realised... You were just a dream to me before...before...' she added huskily. 'And I thought that my dreams were so wonderful, so perfect that they would be impossible to match, but now…you've shown me just how far short of reality my dreams really were.' And then, her eyes filling with love-induced tears, she reached for his hand, tenderly placing it against her lips as she whispered a tremulous, 'Thank you. Thank you so much my love…my true love…my only love…'

If it hurt a little that he didn't return her words of love to him with his own to her, Annie reminded herself that he had just *shown* her how he felt, just physically revealed his emotions, his love, and that men were notoriously shy of putting their emotions into words.

Her last thought before she fell asleep was that she was the most fortunate woman who had ever lived.

As he looked down into Annie's peacefully sleeping face, Dominic Carlyle wondered grimly how she could possibly sleep so peacefully, so apparently guiltlessly and innocently.

Angrily he turned away from her and reached for his discarded clothes.

Well, *she* might be sleeping happily, but there was no way he could. What on earth had possessed him? She no longer meant anything to him emotionally. How could she? His eyes closed, his mouth momentarily compressing as he had an unwanted memory of the look in her eyes just before she had finally fallen asleep, worn out by their lovemaking…just after she had made that extraordinary gesture of reaching for his hand. He swallowed fiercely. It had just been a piece of play-acting, that was all, like everything she had done. It had to have been—there was no other way he could either understand or account for her extraordinary behaviour.

As he walked naked towards the bedroom door, his discarded clothes in one hand, he paused to turn his head and look back towards the bed and Annie's sleeping figure. She was lying facing him, her body curled up as though it was still curled against his own. A savagely contemptuous smile twisted his mouth. Even in her sleep she had to go on pretending... *Why? What* had made her do it? All that idiotic stuff about fate she had come out with...all that... Quickly he stopped, reminding himself that there was only one way he was going to find out the truth and that was by asking Annie herself.

As he opened the bedroom door and headed for a spare room he was shaking his head, wondering how on earth she had the gall to do what she had done. To simply walk back into his life and behave as though nothing had happened...as though the intervening years had never been.

CHAPTER FOUR

IRRITABLY Dominic sat up in bed and reached for his watch. Four o'clock in the morning. There was no way he was going to be able to get back to sleep. He felt too on edge, too charged up, his mind too full of anger and memories.

He had scarcely been able to believe it when he had seen Annie in the restaurant where he was being wined and dined by the executives of Petrofiche, in celebration of his acceptance of the position they had offered him as consultant marine biologist, and then, when she had actually arrived at the house...

Had she known that he was coming back? He had never intended to keep the house, but his work in the Middle East had kept him out of the country and it had made sense for him to let the house rather than try to sell it at a time when property prices had been in steep decline. And then, when he had finally acknowledged that he would be an idiot to turn down what he knew would be a dream-come-true career opportunity simply because it would bring him back to the place where he had first met Annie, he had acknowledged that it made sense to move back into the house himself now that the tenants had left.

How on earth had she, Annie, been able to walk back into his life like that? And not just his life. His body started to heat as he remembered the intensity of their recent lovemaking. No, not lovemaking, he corrected himself sternly. What *they* had just shared…what they had just *done*…had simply been an act of release. Sex…that was all. Annie… He closed his eyes, his mouth sad.

She had behaved tonight, talked tonight, as though… As though *what*? He moved uncomfortably in the bed, the bedclothes an irritating reminder of the softness of her against his naked skin, an unwanted reminder… All that rubbish she had spoken about fate and loving him. She couldn't possibly have expected him to believe… She couldn't possibly have thought…

Throwing back the bedclothes, he swung his feet to the floor and then walked naked across to the window. Like those of the bedroom he had left Annie in, it looked out across land secluded enough for him not to need to worry about his nakedness.

Annie!

It was almost exactly five years since they had first met. She had been eighteen and he had been a decade older, but of the two he had been more vulnerable, the one who had fallen so deeply, so intensely in love with her, virtually at first sight, that he had followed her back to the cheap boarding house where she'd been staying.

She had been confused and wary when he had first approached her, trying to appear worldly and in control of the situation and yet in reality coming across as so adorably unsure of herself that he had ached to take hold of her and protect her, to warn her against the danger of allowing herself to be so attracted to a man like himself.

It had taken him several days of constant visits and patient cajoling to persuade her to go out with him, and then only to a coffee bar, where she had insisted on them sitting at a table in the window. He remembered that whilst a part of him had applauded her caution another, the more deeply male predatory part of him, had known that the place he really wanted to be with her was somewhere much more private. But, since he was not in reality a caveman, he had acceded to her uncertain nervous insistence that they stay somewhere public.

They had talked on that first date of a wide variety of different things, the single hour he had coaxed out of her stretching to nearly four, plus the long, long walk back to her boarding house, where he had extracted a promise from her that she would see him again.

Falling in love with any woman, never mind an eighteen-year-old just on the verge of her adult life and her first term at university, had been so very much not a part of his plans for his life that his feelings for Annie had totally confused and shocked him.

Prior to meeting her he had signed a contract committing him to work in the Middle East for the sultan of a small Arab state. In career terms it had been a wonderful, once-in-a-lifetime opportunity—and one he had eagerly accepted.

The few months he had had at his disposal before his departure for the Middle East he had intended to use dealing with the practicalities of letting out his

Wryminster house during his absence and then visiting a few friends who lived in various parts of the country.

Logic had urged him to sell the house—it was far too large for one single man—but, like Annie, he had no close family. The house had come to him via an inheritance from an elderly great-aunt, and out of sentiment he'd felt that he wanted to keep it.

Grimly he turned away from the window.

He had known within a week of meeting Annie that he was recklessly and irreversibly in love with her, and within two that he had no option other than to marry her, much as his conscience had urged him not to do so.

She had been young...too young for the kind of commitment marriage entailed and too inexperienced to judge what kind of a man she really wanted to share her life with. But she had also been alone, and vulnerable, and he had ached with pain at the fear of rejection and aloneness he had seen in her eyes when he had gently told her that he was shortly to leave the country. And the truth was that he had wanted, needed, to commit himself to her just as much as she had seemed to want him to.

The love she had claimed to have for him had turned out to be nothing more than a teenager's infatuation. Was she to blame for mistaking it for something more or was he?

Angrily he started to frown. What was he doing? Even now he was still looking for excuses for her...explanations... Why?

She might only have been a very young woman,

but she must have known that he was not a young boy and that his feelings…his love… She had to have known—but that hadn't stopped her walking out on him without any explanation, without giving him the opportunity to talk to her…to… To what…? To persuade her to stay?

He had been over and over this argument with himself so many, many times before, and he still wasn't any closer to resolving it. If he had been at fault in rushing her into a marriage then surely she too had been at fault for not telling him that she had made a mistake and that she wanted it to end. That way… That way—what? That way he would have used the power of the sexual passion between them to persuade her to change her mind? Would he have done that? Or would he have been able to be strong enough to put her needs above his own and let her go?

He liked to believe he would have done the latter, but perhaps Annie had been afraid he would opt for the former and she would not be able to resist him or the intensity of their shared desire for one another.

And about that there had been no mistake, no error. He had never experienced anything like it before her and certainly never, ever after. But then after Annie he had never wanted to. After Annie that part of his life, that part of him…

Grittily he reminded himself as he recognised and redirected his thoughts. He had brought her back to this house for the first time after a long walk by the river. He had promised to take her back to her lodgings and had fully intended to keep that promise. But then it had started to rain heavily just as they were within yards of the house. Neither of them had had a coat and it had made sense for him to bring her here.

She had been open-mouthed with awe at the sight and size of the house, and he had seen the anxiety and defensiveness in her eyes as she had protested that her wet shoes would mark the polished floor. He had seen, too, and been hurt for her by her obvious feelings of inferiority. In order to try to relax her he had started to tell her something about the house's history and its original owner.

He remembered how fascinated she had been by the dolphins, tracing their delicate carvings with one forefinger, her eyes shining with delight as she turned her face up to exclaim excitedly to him about their beauty.

That had been when he had given in to his feelings for her, totally unable to resist his longing to take her in his arms and love her.

She had been a virgin when he had first made love with her. A girl. But it hadn't been a girl he had made love with earlier this evening. No, now she was a woman...all woman... He could feel his body starting to tense, to react. When she had buried her face against him and started to caress him...

Dominic made a savage low growl deep in his throat, but nothing could stem his memories now.

After their soaking during their walk he had insisted that she stay and have dinner with him.

'What would you most like to have to eat?' he

asked her, and she went shy and self-conscious again, shaking her head and looking adorably uncertain.

He had noticed whenever he took her out for a meal that she always looked to him for guidance before choosing from the menu, but it wasn't until he pressed her for a decision on what she would like on this occasion, explaining that they would need to go out and shop before he could cook for them, that she admitted that her upbringing had not prepared her for the kind of sophisticated lifestyle he enjoyed.

Previously she had talked briefly about her childhood, but that evening she was a good deal more forthcoming—due, he decided, to the potency of the very good wine he had bought to serve with the meal he intended to prepare for them.

His own parents had died when he was young, so their lack of a mother was something they shared. But his grandparents had been comparatively wealthy, and although he had found their care distant, and his life at boarding school formal and regimented, he had never, he recognised, been in the position that Annie was in, of having to be financially self-supporting.

After her admission that she wasn't either familiar or entirely comfortable with the lifestyle he obviously took for granted he was tenderly protective of her when he took her round the up-market delicatessen he drove them to so that they could shop for their evening meal. It touched him to watch her eyes rounding in awe as he picked the ingredients for their evening meal.

It both amused him and brought out in him an

almost paternal instinct he hadn't known he possessed to watch her face as they toured the food store
and he discreetly explained to her what the wide variety of cosmopolitan delicacies were and how they
were cooked and eaten.

'But who will cook it?' she asked him uncertainly
at one point.

Guessing what she was thinking, he quickly reassured her, 'I shall.'

And so he did.

Prior to meeting Annie he had considered himself
to be a confirmed bachelor, a man whose main attention, whose concentration, was focused on his career. It had been his dream from boyhood to be a
marine biologist, and thus to follow in the footsteps
of his parents, who had worked and died together in
a freak accident off the coast of Mauritius.

He liked women. Of course he did. But he con-
fined his activities to those members of the female
sex sophisticated enough to understand that he simply wasn't looking for a committed permanent relationship.

With Annie, though, his feelings had done a complete turnaround. He didn't just want her in his *bed*,
he wanted her permanently in his life.

They came back here with the food they had
bought, and true to his promise he cooked for her,
loving the way her eyes rounded with innocent
delight when he spoon-fed her little tastes of what he
was preparing.

'Aren't *you* hungry?' she asked him naïvely at one
point.

'Only for you,' he returned, watching the way she had blushed, almost dizzy with the intensity of his own desire.

After dinner they went into the drawing room, where he coaxed her to talk about her hopes and her dreams in between feeding her sips of champagne and strawberries covered in rich dark chocolate.

When she had finished eating one, with tiny, delicate little bites, there was a small fleck of chocolate left on her deliciously full upper lip. Unable to resist, he leaned forward to brush it away, smoothing his thumb over her mouth and feeling his body throb deep down inside in reaction to every tiny little tremble of her mouth. When he had dropped his hands to her face, cupping it to hold her still whilst he lowered his head to kiss her, she focused on him with a wide-eyed stare mingled with longing and uncertainty.

'It's all right,' he soothed her gently. 'I'm not going to hurt you...'

Him hurt *her*! Now, Dominic grimaced. What a joke! But he had never dreamed then what was going to happen. She had seemed so naïve, so adorably sweet and loving.

He had taken her to bed for the first time a month after they had met, coaxing her to shed her inhibitions along with her clothes, but in the end he had been the one who had come closest to losing total control, unable to hold back what he was feeling as he touched her, unable to stop himself from smothering the delicate soft-fleshed curves of her body with hungry, passionate kisses.

Six weeks after he had first met her they were married, and two weeks after that she had left him.

He had been totally honest with her from the start about the fact that he was due to take up his new job in the Gulf within a few weeks, and he had told her too, when he had finally persuaded her to marry him, that there was no way he could possibly take her with him.

'So...so how long will you be gone for?' she asked him bravely.

'Well, my contract is for three years. But,' he hurried on quickly when he saw her expression, 'I do get plenty of leave. For instance I will be home over Christmas for a month, and then again in the summer for two. After all, you've got your degree to get and the time will soon pass.'

'Are you really sure you want to marry me?' she asked him.

'Of course I'm sure,' he responded, not realising then that she was the one with the doubts.

'Are you really, really sure you want to marry me?' she pressed him urgently, on another occasion, and again he didn't recognise the cue she was giving him, didn't understand that she wanted him to ask if *she* really wanted to marry *him*.

Instead he told her firmly, 'Of course I am. I love you.'

'But we're so different,' she continued.

'Yes,' he agreed teasingly. 'You're a woman and I'm a man.'

'No, you know what I mean,' she insisted, flushing a little as she told him,

'At the home they taught us that it's the person you are that matters, and I know that that's true, but other people still do judge and our backgrounds are so very different—I...I don't even know who my parents were, and—'

He stopped her then, insisting, 'None of that matters.'

'Yes, it does,' she contradicted him. 'Your friends...your lifestyle...'

'*You* will be my life from now on, Annie,' he overruled her.

'You say that, but you're not going to be here,' Annie reminded him bleakly.

'I have to go. You know that,' Dominic told her, his voice slightly harsh with his own awareness of how much he was going to miss her.

'Yes,' she agreed quietly, and Dominic cursed himself inwardly, firstly for being responsible for her pain and secondly for his own selfishness.

He had, after all, known right from the start of his own unbreakable commitment to his Middle Eastern contract.

He tried to console her. 'It won't be so bad. I know it's going to be difficult for both of us, but other couples manage to survive such separations.'

'Yes,' Annie agreed, even more bleakly, before adding huskily, 'Sometimes I wonder if I'm destined always to be alone.'

'You aren't going to be alone,' Dominic instantly insisted, but her eyes remained shadowed.

'Perhaps it's easier not to have such strong feelings, not to love someone too much,' she whispered to him sadly later on.

Had it been then that she had started to distance herself from him? But she had seemed so happy when they had married, so much in love with him. Or had he, unforgivably, somehow assumed that his ten years' seniority over her had given him the right to know what was best for her?

The intervening years had changed him, he was forced to concede, as had the emotional pain he had suffered. And, whilst he knew he could never understand how Annie had been able to walk out on him without any kind of explanation, the bitterness he had originally felt had changed to a more rational acceptance. But a part of him still needed to have answers to the question she had left in his life.

His thoughts switched back to the past. Annie had married him. There had been formalities that had had to be dealt with, of course—authorities to be notified of their marriage, that kind of thing, and even the rings he had bought for her had had to be sent away to be altered because her fingers were so delicate and narrow.

He had carried her up to bed the first night of their marriage and he had made love to her with the windows flung wide open so that they could hear the soft whisper of the night and the river.

Their loving had been so intense that she had cried out, a sharp, high keening sound of female pleasure which had echoed on the stillness of the night. And for a heartbeat of time, or so it had seemed to Dominic, time itself had seemed to stand still, as though in awed recognition of the intensity of their love.

Afterwards she had cried, and his own eyes had been damp with emotion as well. But the closer it had got to the date for his departure, the more sad-eyed and withdrawn she had become, and mingled with his own agony at the thought of leaving her had been his guilt at the knowledge that he was responsible for her pain, that he had been the one to persuade her into marriage. And then had come the night when they had had their first and fateful argument.

It had been a sultry day, and his own temper had been on a short fuse. He had been dreading leaving her, and the thought had even begun to cross his mind that he might *have* to break his contract with the Sultan and look for work closer to home. But where? One of the oil companies operating in the North Sea?

In the Gulf he would be in charge of a team of divers and biologists hired by the Sultan to check on the effect of pollution on the area's seabed and life-forms. It was a golden, once-in-a-lifetime, opportunity to be part of the kind of research anyone in his position would have dreamed about. It was his intention to publish a paper on his discoveries once his work for the Sultan was completed, and he knew that if he turned his back on this opportunity he would never get another one like it.

But he still hated the thought of leaving Annie. For the past three days she had been crying in her sleep at night, and there was a tension between them that both of them seemed powerless to defuse.

Annie had been due to start her first term at university the week after he'd left, and on that particular day, in an attempt to give them both something else to think about other than his imminent departure, he had spent the evening discussing with her the career options that would be open to her once she had obtained her degree.

'I'm not sure I want to take up my university place any more,' she told him quietly. 'After all, we're married now, and…well…once we have children—'

'Children!' Dominic interrupted her blankly. The issue of whether or not they would have a family was not one they had as yet discussed. The experience of his own upbringing—his childhood belief that he wasn't important to his parents versus his now adult recognition of the demands their work had placed on them both—had forced him to acknowledge that not every adult was up to the huge responsibilities that being a parent meant, and to question whether or not he was himself.

Now he saw that Annie had a completely different viewpoint from his own, and he knew that he had to make her understand that they both needed time to adjust to their relationship to one another before they even began to discuss whether or not they would make good parents.

Certainly there was no question of them having a child whilst he was committed to his current contract. No way did he want a child to suffer through him in the way he had done as a boy—oh, no, no way!

'You don't want children?' she exclaimed in shock. 'But…but why not?'

'No. No, I don't,' he confirmed sharply.

'But why not?' Annie demanded, and Dominic cursed himself for the pain and disbelief he could hear in her voice, setting out as gently as he could to explain his feelings to her.

'Parenthood isn't just about having a baby, Annie. It's...' Desperately he struggled to find the right words. 'It's a very big responsibility. When we create a child we aren't just giving it life, we're giving it...*burdening* it, if you like, with ourselves...with our own personal history. And at the moment I feel that just isn't something I would want to burden a child with. We've got one another...isn't that enough?' he beseeched her, adding almost desperately as he saw the look in her eyes, 'I married you for you, Annie, and not for...for children.'

'Yes, I know,' she agreed, her voice becoming almost pleading as she added huskily, 'But sometimes things happen...a baby is conceived without being planned and...'

'No way...not for us,' Dominic denied immediately. 'I don't...' He stopped, then asked her gently, 'What are we arguing for? After all, there's no way you could be pregnant.'

One of the first things he had done, the very first time they had made love, was to assure her that she need have no fear of him being careless about contraception, and he had been touched and amused when, just before their marriage, Annie had hesitantly confided to him that she had read that sex could be more pleasurable for both of them if he did not have to...to 'use anything', and that because of that *she* had taken the responsibility for contraception into her own hands.

He had let her do it, partly because, if he was honest, he was just as eager to be inside her, skin to skin, flesh to flesh, as she was to have him there without a protective barrier between them.

'We can't have any accidents, Annie,' he reinforced firmly.

'But if we did?' she persisted with unusual stubbornness.

He frowned as he looked at her. Her face was flushed and her eyes unexpectedly determined as well as anxious. It was unlike her to argue with him, and the last thing he felt like doing when they had so little time left together was to argue about a hypothetical pregnancy. He rubbed his temple, where a pounding headache had been irritating him all day.

'*If* we did,' he told her tersely, 'then of course we would do the sensible thing, take the only reasonable option, and have the pregnancy terminated.'

'An abortion!' She gasped and went white. 'You mean you would want me to destroy our baby...to *kill* it...?'

'Annie, for God's sake stop being so emotional,' he demanded short-temperedly. 'When the time comes we can sit down together and discuss starting a family rationally and sensibly. Until that time does come, though, it would be crazy...impossible for us to have a child. Look at you,' he taunted her. 'You're still practically one yourself...'

'I wasn't a child when you wanted to take me to bed—or to marry me,' Annie immediately pointed out stiffly. 'And this is *my* body we're talking about. *Mine*, not yours. And I can tell you, Dominic, there's no way I could ever, ever destroy our child. And if you tried to make me then…then…'

'Then what?' Dominic demanded in exasperation. The ache in his head had gone from a single angry pounding to a pain that was jangling his already overstretched nerves to a rising crescendo so intense that he was having to grit his teeth to prevent himself from complaining about it.

'Then I'd leave you,' Annie told him flatly.

'Leave me? For God's sake, don't be so ridiculous, so childish,' he fumed. 'We've been married less than a month, Annie. You *aren't* pregnant, and…'

'But *if* I were? *If* I were you'd make me have a termination? Right?' she persisted emotionally.

Dominic sighed. 'It would be impossible for us to have a child right now.'

'Impossible? *Why?* Because *you* don't want one? Because—?'

'You know the position I'm in,' Dominic interrupted her shortly. 'I've got my career to think of, Annie, and…'

'Oh, yes, your *career*… I mustn't forget *that* must I?' she demanded, her eyes filling with tears. 'Nothing, *no one* must interfere with your precious career, must they Dominic?'

He guessed then—or at least he thought he had guessed—what was really wrong. Like him, she was dreading their imminent parting, and immediately his heart softened.

'Come here,' he commanded huskily, reaching for

her. But to his chagrin, instead of responding, instead of running to him and flinging herself into his arms, as he had expected, she deliberately took a step back from him, her face and her body freezing with disdain.

'Sex...is that *all* you can think about, Dominic? Well, I'm sorry, but I'm just not in the mood.'

And with that she stalked off, leaving him openmouthed, torn between anger and amusement.

He hadn't seen her display such haughtiness before, nor such obstinacy, he reflected later, when she refused all the tentative attempts he made to coax her back into a more loving frame of mind, and in the end, irritated both by what he considered to be her childishness and his own headache, he shrugged his shoulders, telling her pithily, 'If I were you, Annie, before I thought about having a child I would check on my own maturity...or lack of it!'

That night for the first time since their marriage they slept without touching. Several times Dominic was tempted to reach out and take hold of her, to end their discord by telling her how much he loved her and how much he was dreading being apart from her. But he had a stubborn streak of his own, and an even more well-hidden vulnerability as well, and a part of him needed to have her to be the one to turn to him, to tell him, *show* him, that he *was* wanted, that *he* meant more to her than the as yet unconceived child they had argued so hotly and painfully about.

But she didn't, and in the end, because of the pain in his head, he resorted to taking some of the strong painkillers he had been prescribed for such attacks, with the result that he overslept the following morning.

When he was finally able to drag himself out of his drug-induced sleep Annie had gone.

Gone never to return…

At first he simply assumed that she had gone into the city to do some shopping, but then lunchtime came and went, and then teatime, and it finally began to dawn on him that she might not be coming back.

He scoured the town for her, and the university, empty as yet, but he couldn't find any sign of her.

In the end, in desperation, he visited the lodging house where she had been staying when he had first met her, but the woman who ran the place was away on holiday with her husband, and her cousin, whom she had left in charge, didn't even recognise Annie's description.

He didn't sleep that night, nor the night after, expecting with every heartbeat that she would return. But when?

One day passed, and then a week without any sign of her, without any word from her, and Dominic began to think the unthinkable. Annie had left him, and all because of a stupid quarrel.

She's eighteen, a baby still, he tried to remind himself. Her reaction to their quarrel was excusable and understandable. She would come back once she had stopped sulking. Their love was too strong for her not to do so.

Ten days later, on the eve of his departure for the Middle East, he still hadn't been able to accept that she had actually left him, that she wasn't just playing a silly game with him to punish him. Right up until the moment the final call for his flight was given he still kept on expecting her to appear, to come running up to him, telling him that it had all been a mistake, that she loved him.

And even then he still didn't give up hope, asking the estate agents and the couple he had let the house to to let him know if she should get in touch.

But of course she didn't do any such thing, and in the end he had to accept that the reason she hadn't returned—no doubt the reason she had walked out on him in the first place—was that she regretted their marriage and considered it to be a mistake.

He didn't bother returning home to the UK that Christmas. What was the point? His birthday in March he celebrated alone, and all the birthdays that followed it, along with certain other special anniversaries: the one when he had first met her, the one when they had first made love, the one when they had married.

The years passed, and with them his initial shock of disbelief. All that remained was a natural irritation at not knowing why she had gone without an explanation. He had resigned himself to never losing the hurt, but the last thing that he had expected or envisaged was that she would simply walk back into his life, his home—his bed—as though nothing had happened...without any warning...without any real explanation, without any acknowledgement of what she had done. And he had certainly never imagined

that she would behave in such an extraordinarily
bizarre way.

His body tensed now, as he fought to quell the
surge of aching longing that filled him. In the past,
as lovers, *he* had been the tutor and she the disciple.
But tonight... With the bitterness of the gall that only
a man who has loved a woman more than she has
loved him can feel he gritted his teeth against the
ferocity of his jealousy at the thought of the rela-
tionships she must have had in his absence.

All that rubbish she had talked about fate and them
being meant to be together had just been so ridiculous. Surely she couldn't possibly have expected him
to believe her! So why hadn't he said something,
stopped her—stopped himself? Because he was a
man, *that* was why... She meant nothing to him on
a personal level now—nothing whatsoever—and the
first thing he was going to do when she eventually
woke up was to demand an explanation of her reappearance in his life.

Yes. That was the first thing he was going to do.
And the second was that he was going to get a
divorce!

CHAPTER FIVE

ANNIE woke up with a small anxious start, peering quickly round the bedroom before smiling in relief as she saw the tall, familiar male figure standing in front of the window.

'It *wasn't* just a dream,' she breathed happily.

Dominic stared at her. What the hell was she playing at? Well, he could play as well.

'No, it wasn't a dream,' he agreed silkily. 'And I've got the scratches to prove it. Want to see them?'

As she blushed and lowered her eyelashes in faked modesty he admitted to himself that she was an excellent actress. Even he, *knowing* the truth, still found his heart giving a funny little erratic beat as he fought the temptation to move reassuringly closer to her.

Hardening his heart, he prepared to tell her that she was wasting her time trying to bamboozle him, but before he could say anything Annie pre-empted him, telling him shyly, 'I know this sounds silly, but I still can't quite believe that all this is real. That *you* and *I* are real,' she added for extra emphasis.

'What would you like me to do to prove it to you?' Dominic asked her urbanely. 'Come over there and—?' He stopped abruptly as he recognised that his words, designed to put her in her place, were instead having a very emphatic and very unwanted effect on his own body as his mind agilely leapt the

chasm between his words and the events of the previous night, furnishing him in no uncertain terms
with the knowledge of just how his body felt about
renewing the intimacy they had so recently shared.

His *body* might want her but his emotions most
certainly did not, Dominic assured himself sturdily,
but for some reason he still found that he was moving
closer to the bed and to Annie—because he wanted
to ensure that she had no way of escaping when he
confronted her and demanded an explanation of her
behaviour he told himself firmly.

'I really ought to get up,' she was saying quietly.
'You must have things to do, and...'

'And so do you. What *are* you doing with your
time, Annie? With your life?' he demanded aggres-
sively.

For a moment she looked slightly taken aback, but
her manner as she gathered the duvet around her
body was so composed and quiet that Dominic felt
reluctantly impressed.

'I...I work part-time for Petrofiche,' she told him
hesitantly.

Dominic stiffened. No doubt *that* explained how
she had known that he was returning to the area. She
must have heard on the office grapevine about his
appointment.

'*Part*-time?' he began critically, but Annie didn't
appear to register the contempt in his voice because
she had ignored what he was saying.

'Oh, this is a dream come true for me,' she told
him huskily. 'I never thought... And then, when I
saw you in the restaurant the other night... I never

imagined that this could happen.' As she spoke she
reached out to touch his hand, her expression one of
luminous joy, her whole body trembling openly as
she whispered, 'People say that reality can never
match up to the expectancy of one's dreams, but now
I know that they're wrong. My reality... *You*...'

She paused, visibly swallowing as she raised her
head and fixed her gaze on him, her eyes wide and
dark with an emotion that looked so real that
Dominic had to remind himself just what she was,
and how impossible it was for her to mean a word
of what she was saying.

'*You*,' she emphasised, 'are more, so very much
more than...than I ever dreamed you could possibly
be. I can't believe even now that I've been lucky
enough to find you...that fate should have picked us
out for one another. I feel so...' She paused and
swallowed, her eyes almost purple-grey with the intensity of the emotions Dominic knew she had to be
faking as she continued huskily, 'I feel so, so blessed
too. Last night,' Annie went on tremulously, drawing
his hand closer to her, so he had to sit on the bed,
'was the most wonderful, the most beautiful, the
most perfect night of my life.' She paused, and
Dominic could hear the tiny emotional catch in her
voice before she said, 'You made it that way for me.
I love you so much...I...'

When her voice became suspended by emotion
Dominic reminded himself that she was merely act-
ing...lying...

'Oh, dear,' he could hear her saying, her voice
rueful and husky with self-deprecatory laughter. 'I

think I might be going to cry, and men hate weepy women, don't they?'

He had originally fallen almost as much in love with her gentle sense of humour as he had with her, but, like everything else about her, it was a fiction, he reminded himself sharply now as he made to pull away from her.

'I'm hungry,' he told her abruptly. 'I'll go downstairs and start breakfast.'

It made sense to wait until they were in less emotive surroundings before he confronted her, he told himself as he moved to stand up, but to his consternation, instead of letting him go, she clung tenderly to his arm.

'I'm hungry too—for you,' she whispered, her voice soft with love.

She blushed as he turned to look at her—a soft pink flushing of her skin that, like her downcast glance, *had* to be manufactured, he told himself.

'You want sex?' he demanded angrily, and then, before she could say anything, and without giving himself time to analyse either his anger or the way he was reacting to it, he turned back to her, once again sitting on the bed as he reached for her, wrapping her tightly in his arms, his mouth hard and punishing on hers.

Annie felt almost as though she might faint. To wake up this morning in the bed she had shared last night with the man she loved, to know that he was real, that their *love* was real, was almost too much for her to comprehend. And now to have him hold her, kiss her with such fierce hungry energy, to know, to *see* that he wanted her so much... She ached to reach out and caress him...intimately...but there were still some things, some intimacies she felt too shy to make the first move towards.

And then her hesitancy was forgotten as he suddenly pushed her back against the bed, growling against her mouth, 'You're the one who wanted this.'

'I do...I want you,' Annie whispered back. 'I love you...so much...'

She gave a small moan of delight as he pushed back the duvet, his hand and then his mouth hotly fierce against her naked skin, her naked breasts. In the clear morning light she could see the rosy crests of her nipples, her breasts still slightly flushed and swollen from the night's lovemaking.

As he touched her Annie felt a tremendous surge of longing kick through her body. Lovingly she reached out for him, tensing in shock as he pulled away from her, saying sharply, 'No!'

'You really *do* want your breakfast, don't you?' Annie teased him tenderly as she smiled up at him.

'I'll go down and start preparing it,' she heard him telling her almost tersely as he got off the bed and turned away from her, heading for the bedroom door.

Annie watched him go. Her body still ached for him, and yet beneath that ache lay a delicious contentment, a warm, positive memory of the night they had shared.

The bedroom had its own *en suite* bathroom which she quickly found, almost as though she knew already where it was. So much about the house was familiar to her that in certain other circumstances she might have found her instinctive familiarity with it slightly spooky. As it was she simply felt that it was all part of the extraordinary workings of fate.

Once downstairs, she found the kitchen as easily as she had done the bathroom, this time not so much by instinct as by the smell of freshly brewed coffee and cooking bacon.

'I've scrambled your eggs for you. I know that's how you prefer them.'

Annie stared as she was waved into an empty seat at the table and a plate of piping hot food was placed in front of her.

'I...I never eat a cooked breakfast,' she whispered. 'Only...'

'...at Christmas and other special occasions. Yes, I know,' she was told, her sentence finished for her.

Grimly Dominic watched her as confusion shadowed her eyes and she toyed with the plate of food.

'I can't believe that you can know so much about me without us ever having met,' she began slowly, and then she stopped, a brilliant smile illuminating her face as she told him blissfully, 'I'm so glad that we've found each other and that you love me.'

'*Found* each other,' Dominic derided grimly. 'You can stop pretending, Annie, the game's over. And as for me *loving* you... Just what the hell do you think I am? What kind of *fool* do you think I am? There is only one reason for what happened between us last night so far as *I'm* concerned, and it has nothing whatsoever to do with love. Quite simply I reacted to man's age-old need to scratch a certain itch.' He paused and waited.

Annie stared at him. Her heart had started to hammer shockingly fast, hurting her so much as it thudded against her chest wall that she could barely breathe.

'I don't understand,' she began painfully. 'What are you saying…? What do you mean…? I…'

'Oh, come on, Annie, get real. How much of a fool do you take me for? All that rubbish about fate… My God, but you're a cool one. Walking back into my life…crawling into my bed just as though the last five years have never happened.'

Annie felt as though a huge weight, a huge stone was crushing down inside her, preventing her from thinking, preventing her from speaking, preventing her from breathing, almost. But not preventing her from feeling fear and pain. No, not preventing her from feeling those.

'Please,' she croaked when she could finally force her vocal cords to unlock themselves. 'I don't understand.'

'You don't understand?' Dominic countered irritably.

She could see the way his chest rose and expanded under the pressure of his anger, but her fear of it and of him was somehow distant and vague, as though she simply didn't have the energy, the strength to come to terms with it as she battled with the enormity of the shock she was suffering.

'Do you think *I* understood when you walked out on me…on our marriage?'

Their *marriage*!

Without knowing she had done so Annie stood up,

and then gasped as the room spun giddily around her. In that instant she heard a harsh male voice speaking sharply.

'Oh, no, you don't. You won't escape by pulling that trick on me and pretending to faint. Annie... *Annie*...'

She heard him emphasise her name in raw fury as she finally slipped into the blessed relief of the darkness waiting for her.

When she came round she was sitting down again, but this time in a deep comfortable armchair in a large, pleasantly furnished sitting room. Like the other rooms of the house she had already seen it was somehow vaguely familiar to her.

A horrible, unwanted ice-cold sense of fear was beginning to fasten its death-inducing fingers around the tender vulnerability of her heart. A horrible, unwanted, uncertain sense of...something...

'I... We... We can't be married,' she whispered painfully. 'I...I don't know you. I don't even know your name...'

For a moment she actually thought he was going to strike her he looked so angry, but when she flinched he stepped back from her, throwing back his head and laughing savagely.

'Oh, my God, now I have heard everything. Last night you were claiming me as someone sent to you by fate, your one true love, and now you're trying to tell me that you don't know who I am. Tell me something, Annie, do you make a habit of going to bed with men you don't know? Is that another part of your personality I never knew existed? Just like your propensity for disappearing without explanation? Did you ever once—just once—stop to think how I might feel? How—'

Dominic could feel himself starting to sweat and he recognised how dangerously close to losing his self-control he was getting. He was becoming far too emotional. After all, what could her lack of love for him possibly mean to him now?

Annie could feel the pain welling up inside her, the awful, uncontrollable feeling of having stepped into a world of nightmarish terror, of having all her worst fears made real.

'We can't be married,' she repeated, her mouth trembling. 'We can't be...'

'Do you want me to prove it to you?' Dominic asked her tersely. 'Very well...'

Walking past her, he went over to an antique desk in the corner of the room, pulling open a drawer and extracting a small box from which he produced a piece of paper. He brought it over to her and held it in front of her.

'Read this,' he commanded acidly.

Her heart thumping, Annie did as he instructed. Her blood seemed to be freezing in her veins; her hands were deathly cold, her head light and hurting.

Slowly and carefully, as though she was a child, she read the words written on the certificate, lifting her eyes briefly from it to gaze into those of the man holding it with sick dismay before returning to read it a second time.

'Your name is Dominic,' was all she could say when he started to refold it.

Her mouth had gone dry and her heart was pounding sickly. There were so many questions she wanted to ask him but she was afraid to do so, afraid of his answers.

Twice now he had mentioned her walking out on him...disappearing. What kind of relationship must they have had for her to do that? Instinctively she knew it was simply not within her to walk out of the kind of commitment that marriage entailed. So what kind of marriage and what kind of man...? The kind of man who would take a woman to bed, as he had done her last night, simply for sex?

'I can't stay here. I have to go,' she began unsteadily, but Dominic was already standing over her, blocking her escape.

'No way,' he told her angrily. 'No way. Not until... Not until you've told me *why* you did it, Annie. Why you walked out on me.

'My God, it's the least you owe me, especially after that pathetic charade...that play-acting you put on for me last night. ''I've wanted you so much'',' he sighed, mimicking the emotion of her voice. '''I've wanted you so much...this is fate...'''

Annie winced as she heard the acid bitterness underlying the contempt of his words. What could she say? How *could* she explain. Every word he said felt like another blow to her sensitive emotions.

She tried to defend herself. 'It must have been... I would never...' She stopped, too proud, too shocked, too raw to tell him of her instinctive knowledge that everything she had said to him was true. *Was* true? She wasn't still dreaming about him, was she? Still…

'It must have been…?' Dominic was mimicking relentlessly. 'Can't you remember?'

Annie swallowed painfully.

'No, actually, I can't,' she told him quietly, raising her eyes to his.

They stared at one another in silence for several tautly tense seconds before he cursed and swung round, so that he wasn't looking at her when he demanded tersely, 'What kind of answer is that? What kind of *fool* do you take me for, Annie? You remembered well enough in bed last night. Every little touch, every little word…every single caress and kiss that ever meant anything to me…'

'That wasn't deliberate—' Annie began, and then stopped. What he was saying was too shocking…too painful. She desperately needed to get away, to be on her own and absorb properly what she had been told.

'Hey! Where do you think you're going?' Dominic demanded sharply as Annie took advantage of his lack of concentration and made a bolt for the door, running through it at full speed and almost colliding with the postman as she flung open the front door.

Dominic, who was right behind her, cursed as the postman waved a piece of paper in front of him, demanding a signature for a registered envelope. He could hear the engine of Annie's car firing, and then with a spurt of gravel she was speeding off down the drive.

She had done it. She had got away from him.
Annie was trembling so violently as she drove the
car out onto the main road that she knew she was
not really fit to be driving, but there was no way she
was going to stop now…not until she had got away
from him and was back safely and securely in her
own little house.

Tears were streaming down her face and her heart
was pounding with shock and emotion. She wasn't
Annie White, she was Mrs Dominic Carlyle—a married woman…married to the man of her dreams…

As she finally stopped her car outside her house
Annie was laughing wildly in hysterical shocked disbelief. The man of her dreams… Maybe, but to him
she was the *woman* of his worst *nightmares*!

CHAPTER SIX

'WE HAD a wonderful time. Bob says that we really should try to go again, and I said...' Worriedly Helena stopped talking as she recognised that Annie wasn't really listening to her.

'What is it? What's wrong?' she demanded.

'I...' Annie began, intending to deny that anything was the matter. She was an adult, after all, and surely capable of dealing with her own problems. But two nights of broken sleep coupled with the shock of discovering that she and Dominic were married had taken their toll.

'I've found out why Dominic, the man at the restaurant, seemed so familiar to me,' she told Helena bleakly.

Her anxiety increasing, Helena put down the mug of coffee Annie had poured for her and waited. Getting up from her small kitchen table, Annie walked over to the sink. She poured herself a glass of water and drank it to moisten her nervously dry throat, before continuing shakily, 'He's my husband.'

'What?' Helena stared at her.

'It's true,' Annie assured her, giving her a look of dry-eyed anguished despair. 'He showed me our marriage certificate.'

Half an hour later Annie had managed to tell her the full story of what had happened between Dominic and herself—or most of what had happened! There were some things, some betrayals of her self-esteem, she could not even bring herself to admit to herself, or to tell even her closest friend.

'Have you told him about your accident?' Helena questioned her.

Annie shook her head.

'No. I...I couldn't... He says I walked out on him, and... I...I don't know why he married me, Helena. It's obvious how he feels about me now...'

'What about you? What do you feel for him?'

Helena questioned her gently, momentarily ignoring Dominic's feelings.

'I don't know,' Annie admitted. 'It's been such a shock. I still can't believe...'

'You'll have to tell him about your accident,' Helena told her firmly.

'Helena, I can't,' Annie protested. 'And to be honest I don't think he'd be prepared to listen. I feel such a fool,' Annie told her. 'All those idiotic things I felt and said about my dream man, over and over, and all the time...'

'He was your husband,' Helena supplied grimly.

There was one more very important question she had to ask Annie, even though she could see how distressed and unhappy she was.

'When he...Dominic...told you that you were married, did it...did you—?'

'Did I remember anything,' Annie interrupted her, guessing what she was going to say and shaking her head as she did so. 'No...nothing. I only wish I had, then I could at least...'

She got up from the table and started to pace the small kitchen floor.

'I've got to remember what happened now, Helena...I've got to. Until I do...' She stopped, her voice and face so tortured that Helena longed to be able to comfort and reassure her.

'Why would I do something like that? Why would I just walk out on the man I was supposed to love and our marriage? I can't believe... I've got to know the truth—otherwise...'

'Couldn't Dominic throw any light on why you might have left?' Helena asked her.

'I... We didn't... He was so angry with me...'

Helena could see how distressed Annie was, and she didn't want to put her under any more pressure, so instead of asking her any more questions she started to soothe and reassure her. But privately she had already decided that Annie's husband would have to be told the truth of Annie's accident, and that if Annie didn't feel able to tell him herself then she would have to do so for her.

After Helena had gone Annie washed their coffee mugs, grimly forcing her hands to stop the slight trembling they seemed to have developed. Two anxious nights lying awake unable to sleep were beginning to take their toll on her, but she knew if she tried to sleep now she would be unable to do so.

What you need, my girl, is some healthy exercise—a good brisk walk, she told herself sternly. But deep down inside another voice, sharper and less comforting, was telling her instead that what she needed more than anything else was to be able to remember those lost weeks, that lost period of time. Not until she had done so would she ever be in a position to defend herself against Dominic's accusations, to refute his allegations.

From Petrofiche Helena had learned that Dominic was currently working from home, and she had decided to pay him a visit there without giving him any prior warning of her arrival, just in case he should refuse to see her.

His house and its setting were certainly very impressive, she acknowledged as she climbed out of her car and walked towards the front door. Why had Annie left her husband and her home? Dominic Carlyle held the key that could unlock the mystery, Helena felt sure. Was there some vital piece of information that he was withholding, or was he genuinely, as he had implied to Annie, as unaware of her reasons for leaving him as he had claimed?

Firmly Helena rang the doorbell and waited. She didn't have to wait very long.

'Dr Dominic Carlyle?' she questioned as Dominic opened the door.

'Yes?' Dominic agreed, frowning a little as he studied the set expression on the face of his unexpected visitor.

'I'm Helena Lever,' Helena introduced herself. 'Annie's doctor and friend...'

'Her doctor?' Dominic questioned, his frown intensifying as he invited Helena inside, closing the hall door on the room where he had been working and leading the way into the sitting room.

'Annie doesn't know I'm here,' Helena told him, shaking her head in refusal of the refreshments he was offering. 'But I had to see you because there's something I think you should know.'

Dominic studied her assessingly. She had all the hallmarks of a dedicated and very professional woman. She was Annie's doctor, she had told him, and suddenly an ominous chill of foreboding feathered down his spine.

'She's ill?' he questioned abruptly.

'Not in the physical sense,' Helena responded, equally curtly. The anxiety and concern she had heard in his voice had caught her somewhat off-guard. From Annie's description of what had happened she had expected him to be far more hostile.

'Annie was the victim of a serious road accident which resulted in her suffering from amnesia. Which is why—'

Helena stopped speaking as Dominic interrupted her, urgently demanding, 'What do you mean a serious road accident? We...'

Trenchantly Helena explained, concluding, 'So you see, when Annie told you that she did not know you were her husband she was telling you the truth. She has no memory of the accident or of the weeks prior to it. If you don't believe me there are medical records,' Helena informed him grittily, but Dominic was shaking his head.

He did believe her, but he was still in shock from the total unexpectedness of her revelations.

'Why the hell didn't Annie say something...tell me?' he demanded hoarsely. 'If she had...'

'If she had you would never have bullied and threatened her the way you did?' Helena offered crisply. 'No, I'm sure you wouldn't. No man worthy of the name would behave in such a way, would he?'

Helena could see from the slow dark burn of colour tingeing Dominic's cheekbones and jawline that she had made her point.

'Perhaps I was... Perhaps I did...overreact,' he admitted. 'But do you have any idea what it did to me when she simply walked out and disappeared?' he demanded, when Helena made no response.

'No,' she told him remorselessly. 'But I do know what it did to Annie when she was knocked down in the street and left in a coma, when she came round and it was discovered that she couldn't remember large chunks of her life...'

'When...when did it happen...the accident...?' Dominic asked her harshly.

As she witnessed his reaction to her comments Helena found herself relenting a little towards Dominic.

'Tuesday the twenty-eighth of September, just before midday, according to the witnesses,' she informed him. 'The date and the time are engraved on my memory—after all, I heard them often enough when I sat through the court case with Annie. She had to go to court to get proper compensation for her injuries,' she explained.

Dominic's face had gone pale.

'My flight left Heathrow later that afternoon,' he informed her, adding grimly, 'It's a date and time that are engraved on my memory as well. Right up until the flight was called I was still hoping that she would appear...explain... She'd been missing for ten days by then,' he added curtly. 'You say she has no memory at all of...of our marriage...of me...?'

Helena could see how hard it was for him to say the words, and she could guess how much it would hurt his pride to hear her answer.

'No, she hasn't,' she told him quietly.

'She recognised me, though,' Dominic persisted stubbornly.

'Yes,' Helena was forced to concede. 'In one sense that's true; she did. But not as a real person. Not as...'

'...her husband,' Dominic interjected for her. 'Is her memory ever likely to return? Can anything be done to...?'

'It may return. No one can say conclusively whether it will or not. And as for what can be done... Do you really think if there was anything...anything that Annie could do to remember, she wouldn't?' she asked him, shaking her head.

'When we were talking about what had happened, and about you, she told me that she would give anything, do anything, to be able to remember. I can appreciate how much of a shock this must be to you, but try, if you can, to imagine how it must be for Annie. Not only has she had to spend the last five years wondering, worrying about what the missing period of her life might contain, she now has to contend with the added trauma of discovering that she has a husband she can't remember, who she left without knowing why. I can assure you, Dr Carlyle, that

Annie is simply not the sort of person to walk out on a commitment she would consider as important as the commitment of marriage without having a very, very good reason.

'Perhaps you know more about that reason than you are prepared to say,' Helena probed, holding her breath as she saw the way Dominic's expression changed from one of intent concentration to one of inimical anger.

'I have no knowledge of any kind—secret or otherwise—as to why Annie left. We had had a quarrel, yes, a ridiculous, silly argument about whether we should or should not, at some future stage in our marriage, have children.'

Helena raised an eyebrow.

'You consider the issue of fathering children trivial?' she asked him wryly.

'No, I don't,' Dominic immediately defended himself grimly. 'Quite the opposite. My own childhood taught me the depth of a child's need to know it is loved and wanted by its parents. This was just a quarrel, a row. Caused, I believe, more by the fact that we were soon to part than any real disagreement between us about children.

'How is Annie?' he asked Helena abruptly, totally disarming her. 'I overreacted a little to…to certain aspects of…of her behaviour towards me, not knowing about the accident…'

'She's very shocked,' Helena informed him truthfully. 'But she also has a good deal of inner strength. She has needed to have it, otherwise she would never have survived.'

She glanced at her watch. It was time for her to leave.

'Annie needs your understanding, not your antagonism,' she told Dominic forthrightly. She hesitated. 'I haven't mentioned this to Annie because I don't want to raise her hopes, but it may be that your reappearance might just trigger something that could make her remember.'

Dominic had been in the middle of working on a very complex report when Helena had arrived, but after she had gone he knew there was no way he could go back to it. Although he had tried his best to hide it from Helena, her revelations had shocked him to such an extent that he still wasn't fully able to totally comprehend everything she had told him.

The thought of Annie being hurt, lying in hospital alone, afraid…in pain, close to death…filled him with such anger and pain that he simply couldn't keep still, pacing the floor of his sitting room. *Why* hadn't she said something to him? Told him herself? Why hadn't she explained to him that she was suffering from amnesia? Then he might have understood when she had kept going on about knowing him— about fate. Then he might…

He might have what? It was too late for him to have regrets now, to wish that he hadn't…

That he hadn't what? Taken her to bed? Taken advantage of her? In the light of what Helena had told him his own behaviour was little short of sheer outright cruelty.

But he hadn't known, he reminded himself. He had

thought, believed, that she was simply act-ing…playing him along… Had she really meant what she had said to him? Had she really felt—been reliv-ing—the happiness, the love, they had once shared? Had she really believed that he was her soul mate…that they were fated to meet…that she *loved* him?

Well, if she had believed that she must be thor-oughly disabused of that belief now. Nothing could alter his own belief that in leaving him the way she had she had deliberately destroyed the love they had shared, but that did not excuse his own behaviour. He would have to go and see her, Dominic decided. He owed her an apology for the present, even if she was either unprepared or unable to furnish him with one for the past.

Wearily he recognised that he was in danger of reactivating within himself emotions he had already decided were no longer valid or necessary. But just to think of Annie, his Annie, helpless and hurt, made him feel…made him ache… Made him want… But she wasn't his Annie any more, he reminded himself savagely. She hadn't been his Annie from the mo-ment she walked away from him.

Despondently Annie unpegged the washing from the line, checking automatically that it was dry. She had spent the last hours following Helena's visit in an orgy of cleaning—a displacement activity to stop herself from thinking about Dominic, from worrying and forcing herself unsuccessfully to try to re-member.

She knew that she must have loved Dominic—her dreams alone were proof of that—and presumably he must have loved her, although there had been little evidence of that love when... But, no, she must not think about that. She might have loved him but she had still obviously felt she had to leave him—and then, having done, so had recreated via her dreams an image of him as her perfect lover.

She knew better now, of course, but what she still did *not* know was *why* she should have dreamed of Dominic in the way she had, as her hero, her saviour, her special one and only person, when the reality was so very different.

'You walked out on me. You left me,' Dominic had told her, and she had no defence against this accusation because she had no memory of the events he had described.

Gathering up her dried washing, she hurried towards the house, trying to suppress the feeling of panic that was spreading through her.

By keeping herself physically occupied she might somehow be able to keep her anxiety at a safe distance, or so she tried to reason. She dared not stop, dared not allow herself even to think about the appalling and unbelievable nature of the situation she was in. She was a married woman. She was married to Dominic Carlyle—a stranger!

A fit of shudders ran through her body as her stressed nervous system went into revolt. Putting down the washing, she decided to make herself a cup of coffee. She had just filled the kettle and switched it on when she heard her doorbell. Assuming that her visitor must be Helena, returning to remind her of her invitation for Annie to return home with her, she went to open the door.

The sight of Dominic standing outside on her doorstep was so unexpected that she physically reeled with shock, only her own gritty determination keeping her body rigid as she refused to give in to the wave of sickening panic that swept her.

'What...what do you want?' she challenged him, dry-mouthed.

'I would like to talk to you,' Dominic responded politely, but Annie wasn't deceived. She knew now how deceptive that politeness actually was.

'Well, *I* don't want to talk to *you*,' she told him proudly, her chin tilting as she clung to the half-open door.

A couple of doors away one of her neighbours was walking down her garden path, and out of the corner of her eye Annie could see the interest they were attracting.

Instinctively she wanted to hide herself away from her neighbour's curiosity, and as though he sensed what she was feeling Dominic told her softly, 'I think you'd better let me in, Annie, unless you want other people to hear...'

He was leaving her no alternative other than to give in, Annie recognised.

Unsteadily she walked into the hallway, allowing him to follow her, needing the cool retreat of its privacy and semi-darkness.

Behind her, as he closed the door, she could hear Dominic asking, 'Are you all right?'

All right? She had to stifle the shard-like slivers of her own pain as her chest tightened and her throat threatened to close up.

'I was!' she told him coldly, when she felt in control enough to speak.

They had reached the end of the hall now, and through the kitchen door she could hear the kettle starting to boil. Automatically she moved towards it, tensing as she recognised that Dominic had followed her.

Don't come in here! she wanted to scream almost childishly at him. Don't come anywhere near me. I don't want you here…in my home…my sanctuary.

'Helena has been to see me,' he told her abruptly.

Annie could feel the shock of his words as though someone had opened her vein and let her blood drain away. The feeling was immediate and sickening: a cold wash of emotional pain coupled with a sense of blind panic and shock.

She felt the kettle she had just reached for slipping from her grasp. She cried out in alarm, instinctively jumping back as she dropped it and boiling water cascaded everywhere. She could feel her arm burning where the scalding water had touched it and she could hear herself crying out too. But it felt as though it was happening to someone else, as though somehow *she* wasn't really a part of what was happening.

She could see Dominic moving towards her. She could hear the way he was cursing as he demanded harshly, 'Let me see. You've scalded yourself.'

'It's nothing,' she denied as she fought not to give in to the fierce pull of her own emotions. 'Just a few splashes.' But it was too late. He was holding her arm and examining it, first his glance and then his fingers examining the long scar that ran from her wrist right up her arm. It had faded a lot now, but it was still—in her eyes, at least—something she preferred others not to notice. Her badge of courage, Helena called it.

'Why did you leave me, Annie?' she could hear Dominic demanding rawly, and suddenly everything was too much for her.

The shock she had been fighting to keep at bay ever since he had told her that they were married finally crashed through the barriers she had tried to erect, and she started to cry, her whole body shaking with the force of her emotions. She put her hands protectively over her face, as though somehow by covering her eyes she was concealing herself from him, and concealing too her own shame at her weakness as she sobbed helplessly.

'I don't know. I don't know... I can't remember. I *can't* remember...'

It was as though just making that admission, just acknowledging that weakness, had somehow opened the floodgates to all the pain and fear she had been bottling up right from the time of the accident.

She was shivering, shaking so badly she could hardly stand up, powerless to control what was happening to her. She could hear herself crying out in denial, as though she was being tortured, and then Dominic suddenly reached for her, wrapping his arms around her so tightly that his body provided a blanket that soaked up and smothered her distress as effectively as a blanket of foam might smother a sheet of flames.

'Right. That's it,' she could hear him saying as the shudders started to die out of her body and her tears subsided. 'There's no way you're staying here on your own. You're coming home with me.'

'No!' Annie denied immediately, pulling herself out of his embrace. 'I'm not a child. I'm an adult…a woman…and—'

'And you're also my wife,' Dominic reminded her sharply. '*You* may not be able to remember that you married me, Annie, but we are still man and wife.'

'We can get divorced…'

'Yes,' Dominic agreed. 'But so far as I am concerned, before we bring an official end to our marriage, there are questions I would like to have answered. There are things we *both* need to know…' he reinforced sombrely.

Annie looked away from him. She still felt weak and semi-shocked by the unexpectedness of her emotional breakdown. Breakdown! Meltdown, more likely. The small patches of flesh the water had splashed were still stinging painfully, and she felt dangerously light-headed, almost relieved to have Dominic take control.

'You're in shock,' he was telling her almost sternly. 'We both are, I suspect. This situation between us is something we need to work through *together*, Annie. I have no idea why you chose to end our marriage, and neither, it seems, do you.'

'What do you mean—it *seems*?' Annie challenged him immediately. 'Do you think I'm just pretending?

Do you think I don't *want* to remember? Do you think—' She stopped as she felt fresh tears threatening her. She felt weak and exhausted, both physically and emotionally, and what she longed for more than anything else right now was to be able to curl up somewhere dark and safe, to escape from all the trauma she was experiencing.

'That scald needs attention,' she could hear him telling her.

Tears burned the backs of her eyes.

'Leave me alone. I'm all right,' she told him. But she knew it wasn't true—she felt sick, dizzy, and her vision was starting to blur. In her head she could see Dominic's face—hear his voice—but not as they were now. Through the mists of her own confusion and faintness she tried desperately to catch the fading images but it was too late—already they were slipping away.

There had been a time, when she was first recovering, when she'd wondered despairingly whether she would ever be properly well, whether her inability to remember perhaps signified that her brain had been damaged along with her body. Helena had been quick to reassure her on that point, however, it had remained a slightly sensitive issue for her—one that had underlain her determination to obtain her degree and hold down a proper job.

Now, as she looked away from Dominic, she suddenly saw the blisters forming on her arm and recognised that she *hadn't* known she had hurt herself. Through the faintness threatening to overwhelm her she could hear Dominic saying grimly, 'Right, that's it. No more arguments. *You* are coming home with me.'

The emergency doctor they had seen at the hospital's casualty department might have told them that Annie's scalds were relatively minor, and that it was delayed shock which had been responsible for her near faint, but Dominic wasn't taking any chances. At his insistence she had been given both sedation and painkilling injections.

Now, as he headed for his home, the case he had returned to her house to pack for her stowed in the boot of his car, Annie dozed groggily beside him in the passenger seat.

Loath though he was to admit it, the vulnerability he had witnessed in her today had not just shocked him but also touched a nerve, an emotion he had thought he had long ago eradicated.

Because of this he knew he was behaving brusquely and distantly towards her, but if he didn't... That look of helpless pride and panic he had seen in her eyes earlier had almost been enough to...

It was because it reminded him of how she had once looked at him *before*, he told himself as he brought the car to a halt outside his house.

'Don't move,' he told Annie curtly as she started to reach for her door handle.

'I can walk,' Annie protested as Dominic came round and opened her door and reached inside to lift her out bodily. But even whilst she struggled to free herself from his hold waves of lethargy and weakness were sweeping over her.

The doctor in charge of the busy casualty unit, faced with Annie's protests that she didn't want any kind of medication and Dominic's implacable determination, had given in to the greater force, and now, as Dominic ignored her protests and swept Annie up into his arms to carry her into the house, she could feel herself slipping away into the comfort of a cotton-woolly world of nothingness.

Because of his impromptu decision to bring her home with him Dominic hadn't had any time to prepare a room for Annie, which meant that he had to carry her into his own room and place her carefully in the middle of his own large bed.

Studiously avoiding looking at her, he stripped off her outer clothes and pulled the duvet up over her underwear-clad body.

She had always been fine-boned, her body when he had first known her naturally that of a young girl, but now, although his senses told him that her curves were markedly those of a woman and not a girl, he was grimly aware of the fact that she was only just on the right side of being too thin, her ribs clearly discernible against the pale sheeny flesh of her midriff.

The Annie he had known had had a healthy appetite and an innocent enjoyment of her food that had made his body ache with the certain knowledge that her appetite for sex...for *him*...was just as innocent and enthusiastic. And there at least he had not been wrong. The first time he had taken her to bed—

Abruptly he stepped away. There were some memories it wasn't wise or safe to exhume, and that was most definitely one of them. But perhaps because of its very danger, he discovered, after he had made his way back downstairs and tried to recommence his abandoned work, it was one that wasn't going to allow itself to be sent away unrecognised.

Stifling a sigh of exasperation, he got up from his desk and walked over to the French windows, opening them and stepping outside into the garden. He was behaving as though he still loved her—but he didn't—couldn't—must not!

In the years they had been apart, the years of her desertion, her destruction of the love they had shared, he had used his anguish to ice-burn his feelings, his love, into a numbness he had refused to feel. Today, seeing the pain and fear in her eyes, he had felt the numbness starting to crack apart.

The knowledge that she had been hurt and close to death, even more than the discovery of her loss of memory, touched and hurt something deep within him he had thought incapable of being touched or brought to life ever again. It wasn't love, he reassured himself. How could it be?

No, it couldn't be love. But knowing that didn't protect him from remembering...

Unwillingly he looked up towards his bedroom window. In that room, in that bed—his bed—Annie lay asleep. Annie... His wife... In the bed he had once shared with Annie... His Annie... His love...

Morosely he looked back towards the river. She had loved to lie in bed at night with the curtains and the windows open so that she could hear the sound of the water. They had even once stolen out in the darkness so that they could swim there together, naked in the silent darkness.

She had demurred at first, protesting that the river would be cold and that they might be seen, but then they had started to touch one another and such things had been forgotten.

The water, he remembered, *had* been cold, but *they* had not!

'You look like a god, a river god,' she had told him tremulously, her hands trembling against his body, the cry she had given as his body surged powerfully into hers lost in the heated kiss of eager hunger they had exchanged.

Later that night, or rather early the next morning, she had reached for him in bed, tracing the sinewy muscles on his arms with her fingertips and her kisses and then, for the first time, becoming more demanding, more assertive as her lips had touched tentatively against his stomach before moving lower.

'Promise me you'll love me for ever,' she'd demanded.

'For ever,' he had told her, and he had meant it.

He moved back inside. He was a grown man now, with an intricate report waiting to be finished, and he had no business standing out here allowing his thoughts to drift into such dangerous waters.

No matter how much Annie's present plight might compel his compassion he *mustn't* allow himself to forget what had happened.

'I *can't* remember,' she had wept, and he had actively felt her fear and panic. But until she could remember neither of them would be fully free to walk away from the past—and from their marriage.

CHAPTER SEVEN

'How are you feeling now?'

'Fine,' Annie fibbed quickly, avoiding meeting Dominic's eyes as she stretched across the kitchen table to pour herself a fresh cup of coffee.

She had been here in his house for nearly three days now. Seventy-two hours. Which in her view was seventy-two hours too many. Granted, she had virtually spent the first twenty-four of them asleep, but she had recovered from the shock of her accident with the kettle now and she felt thoroughly ashamed of the way she had overreacted to the whole incident.

It was time for her to go home. She *wanted* to go home. She *needed* to go home, she reminded herself shakily. The realisation, when she had finally woken up, that she was asleep in Dominic's house and in Dominic's bed had sent a spasm of emotion through her that she still didn't feel strong enough to dare analyse.

She felt nothing for him other than anger at the way he had treated her—of course she didn't. But he had looked after her.

'I'm not hungry,' she had begun that first evening, when she had finally recovered from her shock and he had arrived in her bedroom—*his* bedroom, in reality—with a tray of food.

'Eat it,' was all he had said, but somehow his actions had touched her already sensitive emotions, and after he had gone her salty tears had mingled with the soup he had brought her.

'This is *your* room,' she had protested later, when he had come in to remove the tray.

'Our room,' he had corrected her shortly, stopping as he'd seen the way she froze.

'Don't worry, there's no way I want to insist on my husbandly rights,' he had assured her grimly. 'I've made myself up a bed in one of the other rooms.'

'Actually,' she continued determinedly now, but still avoiding looking directly at him, 'I feel so well that I really think it's time I went home and...'

'And what?' Dominic challenged her. 'No! There's still too much unresolved business between us, Annie.'

'I...I have things to do—my garden, the house,' Annie told him, and then stopped as she saw he was shaking his head. 'The neighbours will be wondering what's happened,' she insisted.

'There's no need for you to worry about any of that,' Dominic assured her calmly. 'I've already explained the situation to your neighbours. And as for the garden, I can speak to the people who do mine and ask them...'

'You've explained *what* situation?' Annie interrupted sharply, her heart starting to thump heavily with nervous tension.

'I've told them about your accident with the kettle and I've explained that, as my wife—'

'Your wife! You *told* them that we're *married*...'
Annie exploded in angry disbelief.

'Why not?' Dominic challenged her. 'After all, it's
the truth.'

'But we're getting a divorce,' Annie protested, and
added angrily, 'You had no right to do that. I don't
want—'

'People to know that I'm your husband?' Dominic
interrupted her cynically.

Annie shook her head. How could she explain to
him how mortified she felt about the prurient curiosity she feared she was bound to be the subject of
once people knew that she had a husband she
couldn't even remember marrying?

'You had no right to do that,' she repeated huskily,
before getting out of her chair and pacing the kitchen
nervously and then telling him sharply, 'I want to go
home, Dominic. I want to go home now.'

'*This* is your home,' he repeated grittily, adding,
before she could deny it, 'I had the house placed in
joint names after we got married, Annie, which is
one of the reasons I haven't been able to sell the
place—without your written agreement...'

'You can have it,' she told him quickly. 'I don't
want...I can't stay here.'

'Why not? What is it you're so afraid of?'

'Nothing...*nothing*,' she denied fiercely, turning to
face him as she did so.

'You're treating me as though I'm your adversary,
Annie,' Dominic told her grimly. 'Your enemy. I'm
not. All I want—'

'Is for me to recover my memory so that I can tell

you why I left you,' Annie interrupted him sharply. 'Do you think *I* don't want to remember? Do you think I'm pretending, lying? Have you *any* idea how it feels to be told that you're married...that you've shared a life...a love...with a man who...?'

Annie stopped as she felt the full weight of her own emotions threatening to overwhelm her. 'Of course I want to remember. But I can't,' she told him flatly.

'Maybe not—by yourself. But perhaps with my help—' Dominic began.

'Your help?' Annie stared at him. 'What do you mean?'

'You and I shared those missing weeks of your life, Annie. I can remember them, even if you can't. I can remember everything we did...*everything*—and I think that if we were to relive them...if I were to take you back through them...it just might...*just* might bring something back for you.'

'What do you mean "if we were to relive them"?' Annie asked him warily. What he was suggesting was ridiculous, and of course there was no way she was going to agree to it, but he was obviously determined to have his say.

'Oh, you needn't look at me like that,' he assured her immediately. 'I'm not some kind of weirdo who gets off on forcing a reluctant woman to have sex with him, Annie. This will be a return to the past *without* the sexual element of the relationship we shared. After all, that is something you *haven't* forgotten, isn't it?' he taunted her softly.

Hot-faced, Annie swallowed the angry words of

denial springing to her lips. He was talking about her dreams, of course, and she couldn't deny what he was saying—much as she longed to be able to do so.

'It wouldn't work,' she told him flatly.

'You can't say that until you try it,' Dominic insisted grimly. 'And you owe it to yourself to.'

Annie turned away from him, unable to make any response, knowing that what he said was true and remembering, too, how she had told him herself she would do anything to remember.

'Very well,' she agreed reluctantly. 'But I don't have to stay here...'

'Yes, you do,' Dominic corrected her. 'After all, you lived here with me.'

'Before we were married?' she demanded, her voice betraying her shock.

'Yes,' Dominic told her laconically. 'After all, we *were* lovers, and there was no reason why we should have lived apart.'

No reason, perhaps, but for some reason Annie felt shocked by his revelation.

'Look,' Dominic was telling her, 'you and I had two months together. All I'm asking is that you give me that time now, Annie. Two months, that's all. If, at the end of that time, you're no closer to remembering anything then I'll concede defeat and—'

'And we'll be divorced,' Annie interrupted him flatly.

'Yes,' he agreed in an equally emotionless voice.

Annie knew that she could have pointed out that since they intended to divorce anyway there seemed little point in delaying matters without any logical reason for doing so. But of course there *was* a reason, and she knew perfectly well what it was. Dominic's male pride was still smarting because she had left him. He wanted an explanation, a reason, and he was determined that she was going to provide him with one.

Her own reasons for wishing to remember her past were far more complex. She had dreamed about Dominic as her lover; her body remembered him as its lover. Before he had told her the truth about their marriage, their shared past, she had craved a closeness with him so strong that he had somehow broken through the locked doors of her memory. So *why* had she left him? Her inability to remember made her feel that a piece of herself was missing, threatening to resurrect all the insecurity she had known as an abandoned child. Only this time she was the one who had done the abandoning—why? She had to find out...

'You're doing *what*?' Helena demanded when Annie telephoned her to tell her what they were going to do.

'Dominic says that until I've remembered the past and him properly neither of us will be able to move our lives on,' Annie explained.

'Well, yes, I suppose he *does* have a point,' Helena acknowledged. 'And if it's what you want to do...'

The urge to tell her friend that it was the last thing she wanted to do was immensely strong, but somehow Annie resisted it. Dominic was determined to have his own way and she suspected that not even

Helena would be able to stop him. She was trying to tell herself that enduring the next two months was going to be a bit like enduring the uncomfortable treatments she had had to go through in hospital. The end result would be worth the pain.

'Well, I have to admit that I'm glad you're not living on your own. You're facing a very traumatic time, Annie—and, stubbornly independent though you are, and much as I understand how you feel, this isn't a good time for you to be on your own.

'I take it that a divorce is going to be put on hold for the time being?' Helena continued.

'For the time being,' Annie agreed shakily. 'It's just a temporary delay, that's all.'

Just a temporary delay. Just two months' delay. But no less than three days into it Annie was beginning to bitterly regret allowing Dominic to persuade her to agree to his plan.

Both Helena and Dominic were insisting that she was still not fully recovered and must not overdo things, and Annie was beginning to feel that time was hanging too heavily on her hands. Dominic, though, had been so busy that she had barely seen him—a fact for which she *ought* to be thankful, she knew, but somehow she wasn't. She felt tired and headachy, her lethargy caused, she knew, as much by the fact that she was not sleeping properly as much as anything else. She was reluctant to allow herself to go into a deep, restful sleep because she was so afraid she might dream about Dominic.

Dominic!

Living here with him was putting her under immense strain, and not *just* because of their shared past.

Just thinking about him made her body tense, a tiny convulsive shudder gripping her. She was far too physically aware of him. Far too physically vulnerable to him. There, she had forced herself to admit what she had been fighting so hard to hide from and deny these last few days. She had brought out into the open her own fear. Physically, she was…she found…she wanted… Closing her eyes, Annie willed herself to bring her chaotic thoughts and feelings to order. It was warm out here in the garden, with the sun beating down on her closed eyelids. Dominic was at work and she was on her own. A bee buzzed busily in the roses nearby.

The roses. She could smell their scent. A prickle of sensation ran through her body. Behind her closed eyelids she could see zig-zagging confusing images: roses flushed with the sun and heavily petalled, their scent filling her nostrils, but still unable to eliminate the sensually thrilling slightly musky scent of the man beside her. She could see his hand, his fingers as he reached for one of the roses.

'No, don't pick it,' she whispered to him. 'It will live longer out here…'

'You're such a baby…'

The warm indulgent sound of his voice echoed against her ears like the sound of the sea heard in a shell, audible, recognisable, but somehow at a distance.

She could feel his breath against her skin, her

mouth, as he leaned closer to her, and she held her own breath, knowing he was going to kiss her, her stomach muscles tensing on a shock-surge of excitement and anticipation.

His mouth feathered delicately against hers, the touch of his lips as light and delicate as the warm air against the roses, but she still quivered in mute delight. She could feel his hands moving up her arms, cupping the balls of her shoulders. Instinctively she moved closer to him whilst his tongue probed the softly closed line of her lips, as busily determined to taste her sweetness as the bee seeking the roses' honeyed pollen-dusted centre.

Her whole body quivered, her response mute no longer as she gave a soft moan of delirious pleasure.

'Dominic...'

Abruptly Annie opened her eyes. Where she had been pleasantly warm and relaxed she was now icily cold and tense, and yet despite the shivers shuddering through her she could feel sweat beading her forehead.

What was happening to her? Was she going mad, or was what she had just experienced a flashback to reality, the sharply jagged edge of a memory forcing its way into her conscious awareness?

Had Dominic once kissed her here, in this secluded rose garden?

'Annie?'

When she heard Dominic's voice she tried to compose herself, but as he looked at her and she saw his expression she knew she had not succeeded.

'What is it? What's wrong?' he demanded sharply as he reached her.

He made an imposing figure, standing there in his office suit and a crisp white shirt, looking both formidable and yet somehow virilely male at the same time. Or was it her own memories that were making her see him like that? Her memories... Automatically Annie closed her eyes.

'I...I think I may just have remembered something,' she heard herself admitting shakily.

Why had she said that? Why had she said anything? But it was too late now to regret her impulsiveness. Dominic was next to her, one hand reaching out to hold her arm as he exclaimed, 'You have? What? Tell me...'

'It was nothing...not really,' Annie started to deny it, reluctant now to describe to him the very sensual and intimate nature of her experience.

'You're lying,' Dominic challenged her. 'Tell me, Annie. I have a right to know.'

Annie swallowed. She was beginning to feel slightly giddy and disorientated—because of the heat or because of what had happened? She could feel herself beginning to tremble.

'I'm sorry,' she heard Dominic apologise unexpectedly as he felt her body tremor beneath his touch. 'I didn't mean to sound so aggressive.'

His apology melted Annie's resistance. Hesitantly she tried to tell him what had happened, beginning, 'It was the roses... I could smell them, and then suddenly...' She stopped and looked at him, unaware of the apprehension and the appeal Dominic could see so clearly in her eyes.

'Was there ever a time...?' she began uncertainly. 'Did we...?'

Dominic knew immediately what she was trying to ask.

'You loved this part of the garden,' he told her quietly. 'You often used to come here and...' He paused and looked away from her. 'I know how difficult and painful this must be for you, Annie,' he told her, in a much less controlled tone of voice. 'But unlike you I *do* have my memories of our time together and...'

He stopped, his hand dropping away from her arm. Oddly Annie discovered that she missed its warmth. Awkwardly she raised her own hand, without realising what she was doing, her eyes widening as Dominic looked at it and then reached out and clasped it with his, entwining his fingers with hers and keeping his gaze on their entwined clasped hands as he continued.

'I'm not altogether immune to those memories of that time...'

Annie could see his chest rise and fall as he took a steadying breath.

'It was here that I told you I wanted to take a mental photograph of you, to take with me when I left, and here that...'

'...that you kissed me and said that my skin smelled sweeter than any rose ever could,' Annie finished, shakily and gravely.

There was a small silent pause before Dominic nodded his head and said bleakly, 'Yes.'

'I...I've only just remembered that bit...when you told me about the photograph. Before I could only remember how you...that you had kissed me here,' Annie heard herself confiding.

'Yes. I kissed you here,' Dominic was agreeing. 'And you kissed me back, and... Oh, God, Annie...'

Suddenly she was in his arms and his mouth was on hers, and the kiss they were sharing was anything but a mere memory.

She ought to stop him, Annie knew, but instead her lips were clinging eagerly to his, and this time the warm sensual scent of man, of him, which was doing so much to destroy her self-control, was in no way imaginary—and perhaps because of that was having a much more dangerous effect on her senses.

Was it because of what she had remembered that she was feeling like this, that she was responding to him like this, wanting him like this? Annie wondered dizzily as his tongue-tip probed her lips and they parted for him.

'Dominic. Dominic...Dominic...' She was even unaware of saying his name until she heard him respond rawly against her mouth,

'Yes. Yes... I'm here...' And then his hands were cupping her face as his tongue probed deeper and more intimately, and their bodies clung and melded together as though they were, in reality, still lovers.

Some things could never be forgotten or wiped out. Some feelings...some needs... Annie's heart thudded frantically against her ribs as her legs parted automatically to make way for the tautness of Dominic's thigh. Instinctively she leaned into him, shivering with pleasure.

Soon he would kiss her throat, and then her breasts, gently peeling away her clothes so that he was free to do so... He would tell her that she was beautiful beyond compare, and her nipples would tighten into two hard, excited, imploring buds that he would suckle into full flower and then...

'No!' Her voice high and sharp with panic, Annie broke the kiss and pulled away.

For a split second she and Dominic stared at one another in shared anguish and shock, and then, equally immediately, both of them threw up protective shutters of wariness to conceal from one another their thoughts and feelings.

'You shouldn't have done that—' Annie began, but Dominic stopped her, interrupting her tersely.

'You shouldn't have let me,' he countered.

Let him! At least he hadn't said she shouldn't have responded to him, Annie tried to comfort herself.

Suddenly she felt very cold and tired, and as though he sensed it Dominic said almost gently, 'Look, I appreciate how difficult this must be for you. But it isn't exactly easy for me either, you know.

'No,' Annie agreed shakily. 'But at least you can remember about...about us. I...' Tears filled her eyes, her voice becoming gruff with the frustration of her feelings. 'You're back earlier than I expected,' she told him, changing the subject.

'It's a nice afternoon. I thought you might feel like

going out,' he told her. 'But if you aren't feeling well…'

'I'm fine,' Annie told him untruthfully. She still felt dizzy and slightly disorientated, but whether that was because of what she had remembered of the past or because of what she felt now, here, in the present, when Dominic had kissed her, she didn't know. And neither did she want to know. Because she was afraid of what she might have to confront?

'Perhaps now that you have remembered something this might be a good time to see if you could remember a little bit more,' Dominic suggested quietly.

'What do you mean?' Annie challenged him warily. If he was going to suggest that he kissed her again then there was no way she was going to go along with his suggestion, but when he answered her sharp query his voice was gently reassuring.

'I thought we might go out for a drive, revisit some of the places we went when we were… together. It might just help to jog your memory.'

Cautiously Annie examined his suggestion.

'Do you really…? I suppose it won't do any harm,' she admitted grudgingly. She might not be sure that she wanted to go along with Dominic's suggestion, but she *was* sure that she didn't want to stay here in the intimacy of the rose garden with him.

At least there could be no memories associated with Dominic's car, she acknowledged with a small sense

of relief as she reached for her seat belt. This was a
new model and...

'What kind of car did you have...then?' she asked
him, suddenly curious in spite of herself.

'Then?' he questioned as he eased the large BMW
out into the traffic on the busy road. 'You mean when
you and I first met?'

Annie nodded her head.

'You can't remember?' he pressed her.

She started to shake her head, and then, for some
reason, she had a mental image of a rather battered
four-wheel drive vehicle, its dark green paintwork
mud-spattered and scratched.

'Was it a...? No! I can't remember,' she told him
shortly.

Immediately Dominic sensed that she was fibbing.
Well, two could play at *that* game.

'It was a small sports model,' he told her, casually
and untruthfully. 'Bright red...'

'What?'

'You look surprised,' Dominic told her. 'Why?
What kind of car did you expect me to have had?'

'Er...I don't know,' Annie told him, shrugging as
she said uncertainly, 'I thought perhaps a Land
Rover, or something of that type.'

'A Range Rover,' Dominic corrected her softly. 'A
dark green Range Rover...'

They were driving through the town now, and into
the town square, where Dominic swung the car into
a parking space. 'Come on,' he told Annie, 'We're
going for a walk.'

*   *   *

'Well?' Dominic demanded half an hour later, his hand very firmly clasping hers as he walked Annie for the third time along the narrow street where he told her they had first met.

'No,' she told him truthfully. 'Nothing. There's *nothing*.'

As she saw the look of disappointment in his eyes her own emotions filled her eyes with defeated tears.

'Do you think any of this is *easy* for me?' she challenged him. 'I *dreamed* about you,' she told him helplessly. 'I thought you were my *dream* lover. But *this* isn't a dream, it's a nightmare, and it's horrible, unbearable...and I don't want it...'

'Just like you don't want me?' Dominic suggested.

Annie didn't dare to look at him.

'This isn't going to work,' she said shakily instead. Out of the corner of her eye she could see a young couple walking towards them, the girl nestled up against her boyfriend, his arm protectively holding her close. Just as they drew level with Annie and Dominic they paused, stopping to kiss one another, lightly at first and then with increasing passion. The girl pulled away first, laughing breathlessly. Transfixed, Annie was unable to look away from them, the girl's laughter seemed to echo inside her head, making her feel giddy.

'Annie?'

She could hear Dominic calling her name and somehow forced herself to focus on him, dragging her gaze away from the young couple.

'I'm tired, Dominic,' she told him. 'I want to go home...'

A little to her surprise he didn't press her to stay, or make any further unkind comments, but instead of driving back to the house he drove out of town and through country lanes to a small pub she had visited on a couple of occasions with Helena and Bob. It was well known for its excellent home-cooked food but there was no way she could ever have visited it with Dominic because it had opened as an eating place only two or three years previously.

'We never came here,' she told him positively.

'No, I know,' he responded. 'But we both need something to eat and I thought it might help for us to be on mutually unfamiliar territory.'

I'm not hungry, she wanted to say. But suddenly, surprisingly, she was.

Their meal, accompanied by a couple of glasses of wine, had had the inevitable effect of relaxing her—perhaps a little too much, Annie acknowledged a couple of hours later when she opened her eyes to discover that she had fallen asleep whilst Dominic had been driving her home.

'Are you feeling okay?' he asked her as she focused bemusedly on him.

Perhaps it was the male amusement she could see in his eyes, or perhaps it was the certain something she felt she could see behind it. Annie didn't know. What she did know, though, was that his air of male superiority somehow irritated her.

'Yes, I'm fine,' she snapped, quickly sitting upright in her seat. 'A couple of glasses of wine doesn't turn me into...a...a drunk.'

'No,' he agreed, his mouth suddenly quirking up at the corners and his eyes gleaming with a look that sent a thrill of sharply warning emotion flashing through her body. 'But if my memory serves me right, and I know it does, what it does turn you into is a delightfully uninhibited and loving woman who—'

'Stop it!' Annie commanded him shakily, immediately putting her hands up to her ears to blot out the sound of his voice. She was feeling vulnerable enough as it was, without him making things even worse. Without waiting to see what effect her distress might have had on him, Annie reached for her door handle and opened the door of the car, hurrying towards the front door of the house.

She had almost reached it when Dominic caught up with her, his hand reaching for her as, to her astonishment, he apologised quietly, 'I'm sorry. I shouldn't have said that.'

'No. You shouldn't,' Annie agreed shakily, and then, urged on by her own sense of fair-mindedness, she added truthfully, 'I know how anxious you are for me to regain my memory, but making digs at me about things you can remember that I can't, in the hope of reactivating my memory...'

There was a small pause whilst Dominic unlocked the door, and then as Annie made to step through it he totally confounded her by saying softly, 'Who says it was your *memory* I was hoping to reactivate?'

He had been drinking too, she reminded herself as she struggled to find an explanation for his extraordinary statement. Even if he had only had one glass to her two, and even though he had always had a much harder head for alcohol. She could remember well how he'd used to urge her to finish her first glass whilst he had been on his... She stopped dead in the hallway. She *could* remember. Unsteadily she walked towards the kitchen, where she could see Dominic filling the kettle and then reaching for two coffee mugs.

'Okay, okay, I know I shouldn't have said that,' he began as she walked into the room, but then, the moment he saw her face, he stopped and put down the coffee mugs, walking quickly towards her and taking hold of her gently as he asked quietly, 'What is it? What's happened?'

Too bemused to question how he could so instinctively know that something *had* happened, Annie replied shakily, 'I'm not sure. It's...' She stopped and looked up into his face, her eyes wide and dark, huge with a heart-touching mixture of pride and apprehension as she told him uncertainly, 'It's nothing, really... Just...'

When she stopped she could feel his fingers tightening a little on her arms, communicating to her his own tension. 'I remembered that I was always still on my first glass of wine whilst you were finishing your second.' As she saw him frown she tried to explain. 'It was... I could see you...us...' she told him huskily. 'I could *hear* you... It was almost as though I was actually there...

'You're disappointed?' she guessed when he didn't speak. 'I'm sorry. I...'

'No, no...' Dominic was quick to reassure her. 'You mustn't be. I'm not... It's a start.'

'Yes,' she agreed a little bleakly as he released her arms. It was obvious that he had hoped she might have remembered more, and she herself was beginning to wish that she had...that she could... Her head had started to ache. Because of the wine?

She wished he wouldn't be so nice to her, so understanding. She far preferred it when he was angry and antagonistic towards her. That way... That way what? That way she could refuse to acknowledge those unwanted tendrils of emotion and longing that were beginning to curl their way around her heart? She was just suffering from confusion...*delusion*...imagining that...subconsciously remembering that they had once loved one another. But that had been in the past, a past that she couldn't remember...a past where she had walked out on him and that love.

'I'm tired,' she told him unsteadily. 'I think I'll go straight to bed.'

Dominic watched her walk away from him, his forehead furrowed in a small frown. She looked so vulnerable, so lost and sad, that he wanted to run after her, to sweep her into his arms and tell her not to worry, that the past didn't matter, that they could... That they could what? Start again? What the hell was he thinking? Just because he had seen her earlier as the girl she had been...just because when he had kissed her she had responded to him...reminded him...

But it wasn't *that* girl who had moved him to remorse and filled him with tenderness just now—was it?

So he still had feelings for her...still reacted to her? Still wanted her, dammit. So what? He was allowed to be *human*, wasn't he? And besides, none of that meant...

None of that meant what? That he was falling in love with her all over again? As a woman this time and not a girl.

He took a mouthful of his coffee and grimaced. It tasted sharp and bitter. Irritably he poured it away. Wasteful, perhaps, but better that than suffering the inevitable after-effects of drinking it so strong: the insomnia, the heartburn...

Heartburn? Oh, yes, he had suffered enough of that...more than enough!

CHAPTER EIGHT

RESTLESSLY Annie looked across the darkened bedroom to the window and then at her watch. It was just gone two in the morning and she had been awake for well over an hour, her thoughts racing round inside her head in an exhausting chase that led nowhere.

The recovered fragments of her lost memory taunted her, defying her to make proper sense of them, their real meaning tormentingly eluding her.

Somewhere deep inside her subconscious lay the answer to the question both she and Dominic wanted so desperately to have answered. But she was no closer to discovering just what it was. The brief memories of her marriage she had regained had only reinforced what her dreams had already told her—namely that her body yearned for Dominic as its lover, its mate, and that whatever her reason had been for leaving him—and it must have been a very strong and important one—it had not been strong or important enough to destroy her desire for him...

Her desire?

Impatiently she pushed back the bedcovers and slid her feet to the floor. There was no way she was going to sleep now. She might as well go downstairs and make herself the cup of tea her parched throat was crying out for.

A rueful smile curled her mouth as she reached for the familiar warmth of her cotton robe. It had been a present from Helena and Bob, a private joke of a gift, after she had commented on having seen it in a shop window. White cotton printed with little black heart outlines and written messages. For some reason it had attracted her attention. It was a girl's robe, really, rather than a woman's, short and demure, but she still loved it.

As she made her way quietly downstairs she paused to admire the carved balustrade, automatically stroking her fingers along the polished wood. The long months of her recovery had given her time, which she had used in reading and learning…in thinking, broadening her outlook in every direction. The uncertain young girl she had been, defensively concerned that others would reject her because of her background, had been replaced by a young woman confident in herself and about herself.

It still hurt, of course, to know that her mother had abandoned her and that she would never, ever know just who her parents were. But the mutual love and respect that existed between herself and Helena, the rapport and closeness they shared, had shown her that it was as herself that she was valued, *because* of what and who she was and not in spite of it.

In the children's home where she had grown up she had been too quiet and withdrawn to make many friends, or to have much appeal to the couples who had come to the home looking for a child to adopt or foster.

Annie paused as she reached the bottom of the

stairs, her forehead pleating in a small frown as she remembered one particularly painful incident from her childhood.

She had been about four at the time, one of two little girls being considered for adoption by a young couple who had already visited the home on several occasions. Annie had hoped desperately that they would choose her, but she had been too shy to vocalise her feelings to them when they had taken her out, praying desperately at night instead that they would choose her. But then had come the day when they had visited the home with an older couple—obviously the parents of one of them, Annie now realised. She had been standing outside the door, waiting to be summoned in to see them, when she had overheard a conversation between them all.

'I like Annie,' she had heard the younger woman saying. 'She is so sweet and pretty.'

'Annie?' the older woman had intervened sharply. 'Isn't that the child who was abandoned? I don't think you should chose her, Elaine. You don't have the faintest idea what her background is—other than... Well, I mean, circumstances speak for themselves, don't they? What kind of person would abandon their child? And you know what they say about bad blood! No. I think you should go for the dark-haired one. At least you know her background.'

As in any structured society there had been a hierarchy, a pecking order in the home, and Annie had already known that she was 'different' from most of the others, in that no one had any idea who she was or where she had come from. She had been found by an elderly woman, wrapped in a woolly jumper in the ladies' toilets at a town's busy railway station, and despite every attempt on the part of the authorities for someone to come forward and claim her no one had done so. At that moment she had known why. It was because she had bad blood!

In the kitchen she made herself a cup of tea and then walked back into the hallway, stopping as she reached the open door to the sitting room.

It had been in there that she and Dominic had cuddled up together in the evenings. Reading...talking...

Shakily she walked into the room, heading, not for the sofa but for the large chair alongside it, carefully placing her tea on the coffee table and then sitting down facing the sofa, staring searchingly at it.

What was she looking for? Some inner vision of Dominic and herself seated there?

She was, she discovered, holding her breath, willing herself almost to see them...to remember more... But already the memory was fading, stubbornly refusing to metamorphose into anything more meaningful.

Angrily Annie subsided into her chair. She felt as though her own memory was playing a deliberately tormenting game with her, feeding her just enough information to lead her on but then refusing to give her something more substantial.

There was a notepad and a pen on the table, and on an impulse she reached out and picked them up, settling back in the chair, curling her legs beneath her as she started to doodle idly.

Stiff, spiky-branched trees...a little house, four-square to the world, with curtained windows and smoke coming out of its chimney. She gave it a garden, picket-fenced and secure. Well, it didn't take much imagination to know what *that* represented. But what about the river she had also drawn, and the car? A large, boxy vehicle, not totally unlike a four-wheel drive—Dominic's Range Rover?

'Think… Think…' Annie urged herself. 'Remember…'

She started to write. Dominic's name, she realised when she had finished, with little sketched hearts over the 'i's instead of dots. Now why had she done that? She wrote down the word 'marriage', and then under it she started to write another list of words, her pen moving faster and faster as she did so.

When she finally stopped she was breathing as though she had physically exerted herself and her heart was pounding.

Nervously she studied the list.

Love. Trust. Respect. Joy. Sharing. Acceptance. Dominic.

Tears blurred her eyes.

Dominic grimaced as he stared at his alarm clock. He had woken up abruptly several minutes ago, as alertly and totally awake as though it was seven in the morning and not still three.

He knew there was no way he was going to go back to sleep. He might as well use the time to do some work. Slipping out of bed, he pulled on his robe.

*   *   *

Annie was concentrating so hard on her list that she failed to see or hear Dominic until he was in the sitting room, and her face burned bright pink with self-consciousness when she looked up and saw him.

'I couldn't sleep,' she told him, almost defensively. 'So I came downstairs to make a drink...'

'Mmm... Me too...' Dominic told her, going to stand beside her so that he could look down at the list she wasn't quite quick enough to conceal.

'What are you doing?' he asked curiously.

'It's nothing...just... I just thought if I wrote down whatever came into my head it might somehow...'

'May I see?' Dominic asked her, sitting down on the sofa.

Reluctantly Annie handed over the piece of paper. 'I don't know why I bothered,' she told him. 'It was a silly idea and... What is it?' she demanded as she saw the way he was frowning as he concentrated on the paper.

'Nothing,' he told her shortly, and then, as though he recognised how curt he had been, he explained, 'It's the little hearts...above the "i"s. Like these on your robe,' he added, pointing out a similarity that Annie herself hadn't recognised. 'That's the way you always used to write my name. You used to say that the hearts were ours.'

He looked back at the list and Annie studiously avoided meeting his eyes when he eventually finished. She was aware of a very special subtle aura of intimacy and closeness enclosing them, as though both of them had briefly let down their defences.

'*What* went wrong between us?' she asked

Dominic helplessly. *'Why...?'* She stopped and took a deep breath before admitting shakily to him, 'Sometimes I feel I'm destined to have unanswered questions in my life, empty spaces...'

Her eyes clouded and Dominic guessed intuitively what she was thinking. Like her, he too was conscious of an unexpected closeness between them, a sense of them sharing their need to discover her lost past.

'You mean your parents?' he asked her.

Numbly Annie nodded her head.

'I often wonder if she, my mother, ever thinks of me.'

Her unguarded admission touched Dominic's feelings in a way he hadn't expected. He was in danger of responding to her as though he still loved her, he warned himself, and then proceeded to ignore his self-warning as he told her gently, 'I'm sure she does.'

It was and always had been his personal opinion that the mother who had abandoned Annie as a very new baby must have been a very young and very frightened girl, too immature and too afraid to admit that she had given birth, and Dominic felt equally sure that as she had grown up and matured she must have spent many sad hours wondering about the baby girl she had abandoned.

'I could never do that to my child,' Annie burst out passionately. 'Never. Not under any circumstances. Not for anyone...' She stopped and flushed. What on earth had provoked such an outburst from her?

'Can I ask…?' she began, and then stopped, before speaking again and very quickly, so she didn't lose her courage or change her mind. 'Will you tell me what it was like for us…being married?' she asked Dominic huskily. 'Perhaps it might help me to remember. I don't know…'

'It was…it was very good,' Dominic told her sombrely. 'In fact…' He paused and looked past her, as though he was able to see something she could not. 'It was more than very good, Annie,' he told her. 'It was…we were…'

As she heard the emotion in his voice and saw the brief sheen on remembered pain in his eyes Annie was overwhelmed with sorrow and remorse.

'Oh, Dominic,' she protested. 'I…'

She stopped and looked at him, his eyes…his mouth…his… Her heart lurched as her gaze was drawn inextricably back to his mouth.

'Annie…'

She could hear the protest in his voice, and the need, and then suddenly they were reaching for one another, touching, kissing, with an inevitability that Annie knew nothing could have prevented.

Annie felt herself being lifted tenderly out of her chair and drawn down against Dominic's body. She had no will to resist him; she could find no need, no reason. She felt his hand tremble slightly as he smoothed her hair off her face. They might have made love a hundred times before, but instinctively Annie knew that this was different, that this was special; what they were feeling, sharing, was not merely a re-enactment of their shared past.

This Dominic, who held and touched her now, was not a figment of her imagination, nor even her husband from the past. This Dominic was the man he was in the here and now.

In the light of the lamp she had switched on she could see his face, shadowed and mysterious and yet at the same time familiar. She traced the shape of his jaw, the curve of his cheekbone, and then stopped as she saw the way he was watching her. Time itself seemed to rock to a standstill—no sound, no movement, no breath even breaking the intensity of their silent communication with one another.

Very slowly and carefully Dominic lowered his head towards her. Automatically her lips parted, her eyes closing in sweet, sensual anticipation. His lips felt warm against hers, their caress so sensitising and arousing that she started to quiver. A soft moan broke the silence between them as his hands slid down her body, shaping the nakedness of her curves beneath her thin robe.

Now she understood why she had been so drawn to its small printed hearts. They *were* almost an exact replica of the ones she had drawn in Dominic's name. She pressed closer to him, her mouth softening enticingly beneath his.

Dominic shuddered as he felt the response of her mouth and her body. Beneath his touch her nipples had flowered into life, and he could see as well as feel their sharp outline beneath her robe. His body was even more flagrantly proclaiming its own arousal, and his tongue was pushing against the flimsy resistance of her softened lips.

What had begun as an attempt to show her just how good their love had been had turned swiftly into something far more potently dangerous, and rooted in the present. The woman he was holding, kissing...caressing...wanting...wasn't the Annie of the past, the girl he had married. The woman he was holding now...wanting now...was Annie as she now was, and the way he wanted her, the intensity with which he wanted her, faded into insignificance his memories of the way they had once been.

He had known already of the danger he was in, and now it couldn't be denied any longer. He *was* falling in love with her all over again, abusing the power his position in her life gave him to use, what on her part had been an innocent and anguished plea for his help to satisfy his own need.

He had to stop before it was too late...before he...

Annie tensed in loss and bemusement as Dominic tore his mouth from hers. He was breathing heavily, and she could feel her own heart pumping fast in aroused response.

'Dominic,' she protested yearningly, but he was already distancing himself from her.

'We shouldn't be doing this,' he told her curtly. 'This isn't... We're playing with fire, Annie,' he told her bluntly. 'It would be the easiest thing in the world for me to take you to bed now, but...'

Annie felt her face start to burn with humiliation, but much as she longed to be able to do so she knew she couldn't deny his assertion. What was wrong with her? Where was her pride? Why was she flinging herself at him, virtually begging him to make love to her?

'You're right,' she agreed proudly, forcing herself to appear indifferent and unconcerned. 'To be honest,' she added as carelessly as she could, as she turned away to pick up the sheet of paper she had been writing on, 'personally, *I* don't believe it matters *why* our marriage ended. Even if I did remember, it wouldn't change anything. I think it would be best if we just went ahead and got a divorce.'

What would she do if he grabbed hold of her and told her there was no way he ever wanted to let her go? Did he *really* need to ask himself that question? Dominic wondered grimly.

Only now did he recognise that somewhere over the last few days his desire to understand why Annie had left him, to draw a line under their marriage, had been replaced by a far more urgent need to discover what had gone wrong in order that he could somehow put it right. It wasn't the past and formally ending their marriage he was focusing on, but the present, and the future he wanted to convince Annie they could have together.

'Best for whom?' he challenged her sharply as the fragile fabric of his hopes gave way under the weight of reality. 'Not for me. There are still answers that I need from you, Annie. And until I get them…'

He stopped and took a deep breath before continuing. 'Look, this isn't going to get us anywhere. I suggest that we will be able to discuss the whole subject more rationally when we've slept on it.'

He was right; Annie knew. Her own emotions felt

strung out, raw and over-sensitive. She ached for him in a way that both tormented and infuriated her. He had no right to be able to make her feel like this.

But half an hour later in her own room, waiting for sleep to deaden the intensity of her emotions, a tear crept down her cheek as she reflected unwillingly on the closeness she had felt between them before Dominic had destroyed it. Was that what it had been like between them? Had they been so close, so attuned to one another, so much in love with one another that nothing and no one else had mattered?

An aching sense of loss and loneliness filled her, a sharply acute feeling of grief and pain as she wept for the love that she and Dominic had somehow, between them, destroyed.

'Tell me again. Everything. All of it...right from when we met...' Annie demanded doggedly.

Dominic sighed, examining her pale set face. They had been treating one another with cautious reserve since the night he had so nearly given in to the temptation to make love to her, and it made his heart ache to see the way Annie was driving herself, pushing herself, to try to regain her memory.

They were walking by the river, and suddenly Annie gave a sharp exclamation as a couple of youths on bicycles came up behind her, sounding their horns and making her stumble in surprise.

Automatically Dominic reached out to steady her, frowning as he felt the way her body shuddered beneath his protective arm.

'Are you all right?' he asked her in concern.

'They gave me a shock,' Annie admitted. Her teeth had started to chatter together and she was trembling so violently that Dominic was loath to let her go.

'You said we met *when*?' she began to prompt him, but Dominic refused to be diverted.

'You're not well,' he told her sharply. 'And I think—'

'I don't care what you think, Dominic,' Annie interrupted him in a high, strained voice. 'All I care about is finding out why I left you and getting on with my life.'

Dominic's concern increased. He was worried that if he didn't take a stand the pressure she was putting herself under to try to remember was going to make her ill.

Every day now, several times a day, she insisted on him telling her the history of their relationship, demanding to know every tiny detail and listening to him with increasing desperation as nothing he said triggered off any memories for her.

'*Why* can't I remember?' Annie demanded helplessly. 'Why? Why…?'

She sounded and looked so tortured that Dominic automatically wanted to comfort her.

'Don't. Don't push yourself so hard,' he urged her, and then as she turned her head he caught sight of the tears on her eyelashes and it was too much for his self-control.

'Annie, Annie,' he groaned as he reached for her.

Frantically Annie tensed against the tormenting intimacy of his arms. His breath brushed softly against her skin and her body quivered helplessly in longing for him. She wanted him so much…loved him so much… How could she deny it?

'No, Dominic,' she protested defensively, but it was already too late, and her lips parted weakly under his as he brushed the tears from her eyelashes.

Obliviously they clung together, sharing the bittersweetness of a kiss that could have been that of tender new lovers. But she couldn't let him guess how she felt. Her pride wouldn't let her.

Somehow she managed to find the strength to push him away. As she turned away from him suddenly the world turned dark and swung dizzily around her.

'Annie…'

She could hear the anxiety in Dominic's voice as he called her name, but somehow she was distanced from it and in another place…another time… She had a vivid sharp memory of another occasion on which she had walked beside the river with Dominic. They had kissed then too, but then… Annie drew in her breath in a sharply painful gasp.

'Annie? What is it? What's wrong? Tell me,' Dominic insisted.

Hazily Annie focused on him. Her mental image of them had faded now. But not the memory it had brought.

'I…we were walking here,' she told him distantly. 'You kissed me, and then…' She stopped and looked back the way they had just walked, in the direction in which the house lay.

'And then I whispered to you that I wanted to take you home, to be where I could make love to you properly,' Dominic supplied rawly for her. 'And you looked at me and—'

'I don't want to hear any more,' Annie interrupted him. Her mouth had gone dry and her heart had started to race. The images Dominic's soft words were conjuring up were making her feel far too vulnerable.

It was only her pride now that was making her grit her teeth and see through her determination to make herself remember. Every day she spent with Dominic, every hour was making her more and more aware of the danger she was in. She might not know why she had left him but she certainly knew why she had fallen in love with him.

Only this morning, in an unguarded moment, he had made her laugh with his droll description of an incident which had taken place at work. And it had disconcerted her to discover that they shared not only the same taste in food but that they also read the same newspaper, liked the same kind of countryside, enjoyed the same TV programmes, felt passionate about the same issues.

'Come on,' Dominic told her abruptly. 'I'm taking you home. Oh, it's all right,' he assured her when he saw the panic crossing her face, 'I'm not about to re-enact our past and take you to bed. If I did…'

He stopped, and Annie stopped too, forgetting the danger of looking intimately at him as she lifted her gaze to his face and felt her heart thump and bang against her ribs in reactive punishment.

'You're exhausted. No, don't bother trying to deny

it. I can see it in your eyes. You're pushing yourself too hard...'

'You're the one who wants me to remember,' Annie told him shortly, but he refused to react to her defensive aggression.

'I thought we'd agreed that we *both* need to know the truth,' he said calmly. When she made no response he continued gently, 'Come on, let's get you home.'

Home! Quickly Annie blinked away the humiliating threat of her tears. She had been so awed, so thrilled—so overwhelmed when she had realised that Dominic's house was to be her home.

'Well, where did you expect us to live?' he had teased her lovingly.

'I... I... It's so big,' she had breathed.

'It's just a house, Annie,' Dominic had tried to reassure her. 'Bricks and mortar, that's all. Only with you to share it with me it can truly become a home.'

A home. *Her* home. The *first* real home she had ever known. And Dominic had gone out of his way to make sure she had felt that it *was* her home.

He had taken her shopping, insisting that she was to choose new decor for their shared bedroom, encouraging her to trust her own instincts and taste. She smiled wryly, remembering the hours she had spent poring over books she had bought, trying to find out what style of decor would be right for the house.

'The Chinese silk would have been wonderful, but I was afraid because it was so expensive,' she said now.

Both of them looked at one another, and then,

without any kind of hesitation, Dominic said easily, 'You mean for the bedroom curtains? Yes, it would have looked good. Especially if you'd given in and let me buy that four-poster bed.'

Annie closed her eyes in despair.

'What's wrong with me?' she demanded in a guarded voice. '*Why* can I remember something as unimportant as the curtain fabric I didn't choose when I can't remember the most vital thing of all?'

There was a brief pause before Dominic replied somberly, 'Perhaps it's less painful to remember why you rejected the silk.'

He didn't say anything else. He didn't need to, Annie recognised. What he had implied was that her rejection of *him* was something too traumatic for her to allow herself to recall, and she knew that he was probably right.

Out of all the questions she had asked him, she acknowledged, there was one she still had not been able to bring herself to ask, but now, suddenly, she felt she had to do so. Touching his arm tentatively, she asked huskily, 'Why do *you* think I left?'

At first she thought he wasn't going to answer her. The bleak expression hardening his mouth made her shiver a little.

'How many times have I asked myself that question?' he said, half under his breath. 'And not been able to give myself an answer. I can't think of any logical explanation. You were upset because I was going away. We had rowed about it. We'd been having a series of petty rows brought on by the tension of our imminent parting.'

'But I knew right from the start that you had to go.'

Annie had surprised herself by defending him. A wry smile touched his mouth. 'You're playing devil's advocate with a vengeance,' he told her. 'I *had* told you, yes, but that didn't stop me from feeling guilty about leaving you.'

'But you had no choice,' Annie insisted.

His mouth turned down at the corners.

'There are always choices. I could have broken the contract. I could have put you first...shown you... You were too young for the pressure of that kind of separation and...' Dominic paused, carefully searching for words that would not anger or offend her. 'Your background being as it was meant that you had more need to feel secure...wanted...loved. Perhaps more than I had made allowance for. Perhaps...'

'Perhaps that made me run away like a sulky child?' Annie supplied grimly for him, adding before he could stop her, 'A sulky child demanding attention and playing up to get it... Is *that* what I was like, Dominic?'

'No. Not at all,' he tried to reassure her.

'But that is what you think, isn't it?' she guessed. 'You think I *did* leave because you were going away, to punish you for leaving me. But that's so childish.'

'It's a possibility,' he allowed. 'You were very young, and at that age it's dangerously easy to mistake a crush for love.'

Annie frowned. Although his explanation sounded feasible, for some reason she couldn't accept it. It jarred on her, rubbed against her own inner knowledge of herself.

'Come on,' Dominic reiterated. 'You're exhausted. What you need is a hot bath and then bed. I'll bring you some supper up on a tray and—'

'Read me a bedtime story?' Annie finished dryly. 'I'm not a child now, Dominic.'

'No,' he agreed. 'You're not. And anyway, aren't bedtime stories supposed to have happy endings?' he asked, in a sharply bleak voice that wrenched at her own emotions so painfully she caught her breath.

There could be no happy ending to their own story. Not unless— Not unless what? Not unless Dominic told her that he didn't care what had happened in the past, that he loved her far too much in the here and now to ever let her go? Was that what she really wanted? What she wanted was him, Dominic—her lover, her husband, her fate, she recognised achingly.

'I've got to go into the office and the chances are that I'm going to have to work late,' Dominic told Annie as he finished his breakfast.

Annie averted her face. The sight and smell of his coffee was making her feel acutely nauseous, and her stomach heaved protestingly, just as it had heaved for the last three mornings in a row. 'Will you be all right here on your own?'

'I'll be fine,' she assured him. The scald wounds on her arm had healed cleanly, without any problems, and even Dominic was forced to agree with her doctor that she was now fully recovered.

Dominic looked across the table at her.

'There's something I want you to promise me,' he told her quietly.

Annie gave a small sigh.

'If I remember anything I promise you I'll tell you about it—' she began, but he stopped her with a shake of his head.

'No, that isn't what I was going to ask.' He made a movement as though he was going to reach for her, and then stopped himself, getting up to go and stand with his back to her in front of the window. 'I want you to promise me, Annie, that there won't be another disappearing act. Promise me,' he demanded harshly when she made no immediate response.

He was afraid that she was going to leave whilst he was gone. Bemusedly Annie stared at his dark-suited back. His shoulders were so broad, his stance so upright, his air so authoritative and male that it was almost impossible for her to believe that he was vulnerable in any kind of way, but his words were telling her a different story.

'If I don't promise?' she asked him huskily.

He turned round.

'Then I don't go,' he told her unequivocally.

Annie blinked in surprise. If it mattered so much to him that she stayed, then—she was letting her imagination and her own feelings run away with her, she warned herself. The reason he wanted her to stay was because he still wanted to get to the bottom of why she had left him.

'I...I'll stay,' she told him unsteadily. As she glanced towards the calendar on the kitchen wall she recognised absently that she had already been here with him for over a month. Over a month! Her stomach started to churn like a washing machine on full spin. Over a *month*! That meant...

Somehow Annie managed to make herself wait until after Dominic had gone before going over to the calendar and frantically counting backwards. Her stomach was heaving, panic and nausea vying for supremacy as the truth hit her in a sweat-drenched sheet of shock. Blindly she turned away from the calendar, her hands shaking as she reached for the telephone and started to dial Helena's telephone number. But then, before she had completed dialling, she quickly hung up.

No... No! She couldn't share her fears with anyone else yet...not yet...not until she was sure. She *could* walk down into the town. It wasn't very far and there was a chemist's shop at the bottom of the hill. It would have what she needed. Because Helena's car was off the road Annie had insisted that she borrow her own Mercedes, which meant that she herself was temporarily without any means of transport.

Three hours later she stood numbly in the bathroom as she stared in sick disbelief at the pregnancy test she had just done. Her second...and both of them were showing a positive result. She was pregnant. Dominic would be— Dominic! Suddenly the bathroom started to sway ominously round her. Instinctively she reached for the shower door to support herself, whispering a husky, 'No.'

A confused jumble of images were forming themselves inside her head: sounds, pictures, *memories*.

Somehow she managed to make her way to Dominic's bedroom before she collapsed across the bed. The shutter which had closed her off from the past, protected her from it, had suddenly lifted, and she knew now the answer to Dominic's question. Oh, yes, she knew!

She was pregnant with Dominic's child. Just as she had thought, feared she might be all those years ago. Then she had been wrong. But now...

Dominic's belief was that she had left him as the result of an immature desire to punish him for his having to leave her...that the love she had claimed to have for him had, in reality, been little more than a youthful crush, incapable of withstanding the pressure of adult emotions. But he was wrong.

Tormentedly Annie closed her eyes.

'You don't want children?' she had asked him then, in shocked fear.

'No, I don't,' he answered with cold emphasis.

She was so shocked, so afraid. For days she had been worrying about inadvertently missing one day of taking the Pill, knowing that a baby so soon in their marriage wasn't something they had planned, feeling overwhelmed by the prospect of everything that having a baby would mean and desperately needing Dominic's love and support. Instead the reaction she was getting from him threatened to destroy her—it was certainly destroying her trust in him.

'But why not?' she forced herself to ask him, never imagining for one minute just what she was going to hear.

'Parenthood isn't just about having a baby, Annie,' he told her. 'It's a very big responsibility. When we create a child we aren't just giving it life, we are giving it...*burdening* it, if you like, with ourselves...with our own personal history. And at the moment I feel that just isn't something I would want to burden a child with.'

Their own personal history. She knew what he meant, of course. He was referring to the fact that they—*she*—knew nothing of her own parentage, of what kind of inheritance, both genetically and emotionally, she might be passing on to her own child. Contaminating it with bad blood... That was what Dominic meant. He was afraid of giving his child...their child...her bad blood.

Annie felt as though a part of her had died. As though a part of her had been broken and destroyed. She had believed Dominic totally when he told her that it was her he loved...that her history didn't matter to him. But he had lied to her.

But worse was to follow. When she tried stumblingly to tell him of her fear that it could already be too late, that she might already be carrying his child, his reaction made her feel literally sick with fear.

'An abortion! You mean you would want me to destroy our baby?' she demanded, white-faced.

'Anne, for God's sake stop being so emotional,' Dominic replied angrily.

Annie moistened her dry lips. She couldn't take in properly what had happened. How, within the space of less than twenty-four hours, with a few short, sharp words, her love, her life, her future, her trust, had all been destroyed—as Dominic would insist on her destroying their child.

Numbly she tried to come to terms with what had happened. Dominic was talking to her, trying to reason with her, coax her, but it was as though there was an invisible barrier between them. She no longer wanted even to breathe the same air as him, never mind be physically close to him. He had claimed that he loved her but he had been lying. He didn't want his child…his children…to have her as their mother. He was worried about the inheritance she might give them. He was worried that she would contaminate them with the bad blood she carried.

Suddenly he was a stranger to her. A stranger who threatened the life of her child—a child she knew she would fight to protect to the last breath of life left in her.

There was no way she could abandon her child in the way her own mother had done her. Poor baby. Why should it suffer because she was its mother? She couldn't stay with Dominic now. For her baby's sake, she had to leave him. Round and round her thoughts circled, causing a whirlpool of fear and pain that sucked her down into its black centre.

That night in bed, she couldn't sleep. Dominic had taken some medication for a headache. Logic told her that her wisest course would be to wait until he had left the country before she disappeared from his life, but his departure was still more than two weeks away and she feared that there was no way she could continue to live with him for that length of time without betraying herself.

Driven by the desperation of her own emotions, she left their bed, packed a few necessities and left the house.

CHAPTER NINE

IT WAS over two weeks since she had left Dominic. In a very short space of time now he would be leaving the country, and once he did... Once he did it was unlikely that they would ever meet again.

She didn't know why she had come back here, to the town where she had been born. She had booked herself into the cheapest bed and breakfast she could find—after all, she was financially responsible for herself now. She had been to the library and re-read the newspaper story written when she had been found abandoned. The old lady who had found her had died many years before, and as Annie already knew there was no way back for her into the past to discover exactly who and what she was. Neither was there any way forward into the future for her now, as Dominic's wife.

She shivered beneath the thin cover on her bed.

Dominic!

She missed him desperately, longed for him despairingly, despite the hurt he had inflicted on her.

It was well past midnight. What was he doing? Was he thinking of her...wondering...worrying...? Was it possible for him to love her as a woman even whilst rejecting her as a mother for his children?

She was still awake when daylight came creeping across the sky.

In another few hours Dominic would be gone. Hot, heart-wrenching tears seeped between her closed eyelids. The thought of never seeing him again made her want to crawl away somewhere and die, but she couldn't. She had her baby...*their* baby to think of.

She had to see him...just one last time... Just see him, that was all... She wouldn't say anything to him—she couldn't. She would just go home and watch him leave—watch him as he walked out of their lives...hers and his baby's...the baby he thought she wasn't good enough to mother.

She was on the first commuter train to leave town, making her slow journey back across the country. In Dominic's car, with Dominic's hands on the wheel, she could have been there in a couple of hours. But there was no direct rail service from her home town, only a series of complicated connections.

She was waiting for the train that would take her on the final lap of her journey back when she made the discovery that her flight had been for nothing, that there was to be no baby.

By the time she had dealt with the emergency of her unexpected period and dried the tears she had cried for the life that wasn't to be she had missed her connecting train.

Numbly she boarded the next one to arrive. There was no baby now to keep her and Dominic apart, but there was still her awareness, her realisation of the fact that he didn't consider her good enough to have his children. If she could catch him before he left she could tell him that their marriage was over, that he was free to find a woman whom he did consider good enough.

The journey took longer than she had expected. The train she had missed had been an express, and the one she was on was a much slower one, stopping at every station. By the time she eventually got off Annie knew that Dominic would be on his way to Heathrow for his flight.

Not knowing what to do, she started to cross the road via the pedestrian crossing…and walked straight into the path of a speeding car.

Shakily Annie wiped the tears from her face with the back of her hand.

There was no point in weeping for the sorrows of the girl she had once been. Crying wouldn't do anything to help *her*—nor to help herself *now*, she recognised.

Her body felt stiff and cold, and when she looked at her watch she was shocked to see how many hours had passed since she had first walked into Dominic's bedroom.

Now, as she looked around it, she knew *exactly* how it had felt to lie here in Dominic's arms. *Exactly* how it had felt to be loved by him and to have loved him in return. To *have* loved him? She could still taste the bitterness of her own weak tears. No wonder she had found it impossible to destroy the feelings of love she had increasingly begun to feel for him. The reality was that she had never *stopped* loving him…not for one moment.

'You left me,' he had accused her, but the truth was that *he* had abandoned *her*.

She would have to tell him just what she had discovered, of course. He had a right to know... About the past, yes, but not about the present and the baby she knew for sure she was carrying this time. No, that was her concern and hers alone, and she intended it to remain that way. He had been right then, in calling her immature and a child, but she wasn't either of those things any more. She was an adult, a woman and as such she had no need of any man to help her bear the responsibility of the new life growing inside her.

She closed her eyes, determined not to allow herself to cry any more tears. What was the point?

Logically, she knew she should wait until Dominic returned home to tell him what she had remembered, but anxiety, and a certain instinct that if she was alone with him too long he might somehow discern that she was keeping something vital from him, urged her to get the whole thing over and done with as quickly as she could.

She would pack her things, get a taxi to take her to Dominic's office and then go straight on to her own home.

Grimly Dominic stared out of his office window. For all the good he was doing at work he might as well have stayed at home, because that was where his thoughts were—at home with Annie. Annie... His wife... His woman... The woman who had left him... His *love*...

It was no use. Grittily Dominic forced himself to face the self-knowledge he had been trying to avoid. He still loved Annie. Loved her even more as a woman than he had done as a girl—if that was possible.

In maturity she had become so much more of everything she had already been. He had to see her, talk to her…tell her how he felt and if, after that, she still wanted her freedom…

Quickly he strode out of his office, heading for the exit.

Leaving the taxi driver waiting for her in the car park, nervously Annie started to make her way across it, heading for the main office of the building. It was five o'clock, and staff were already starting to leave, streaming out of the building. Suddenly Annie froze as she saw Dominic amongst them.

'Dominic!' She said his name under her breath, so totally fixated on him that her senses couldn't register anything else. 'Dominic…'

Some instinct he couldn't name made Dominic turn his head.

'Annie…'

What was she doing *here*? He started to move towards her. She was standing, staring rigidly at him.

'Annie!' He called her name, and then cursed as she suddenly seemed to shudder, a statue coming to life.

'Annie…'

Out of the corner of his eye Dominic saw the car, and realised that Annie was standing right in its path, oblivious to its presence or her own danger. With a superhuman burst of speed he reached her, pulling her down on top of him as he fell to the ground and rolling her out of the way of the car's front wheels.

As he did so he felt the sharp thud of metal striking his own body and grunted in surprise. His body felt oddly numb...but somehow heavy... Somewhere in the distance he could hear screams...voices...the wails of a siren.

'Ah, so you're back with us again. Good, I'll go and tell Dr Spears.'

Hazily Dominic focused on the smiling nurse standing beside his bed.

'You've been sleeping for so long we thought we'd start to call you Rip Van Winkle,' she told him cheerfully as she pressed the bell above his head.

Where the devil was he? What was going on? And then abruptly Dominic remembered, struggling to sit up and ignoring both the admonishment of the nurse and the pain in his side as he demanded anxiously, 'Annie, my wife. Is she...?'

'She's fine.' The nurse smiled. 'And before you ask, so is the baby.'

'The baby? The *baby*...' Dominic could feel his heart starting to thud with heavy, adrenalin-fuelled beats.

'Oh, that's sent your pulse-rate up,' the nurse commented, examining the screen on the far side of the bed. 'Your wife was lucky that you had the forethought to do what you did. Otherwise it might have been a very different story, both for her and the baby.'

Annie was pregnant!

Dominic closed his eyes, his body suddenly drenched in sweat as he realised what he might have lost.

'Where is Annie…my wife…?' he asked thickly.

'Dr Spears sent her home. She didn't want to go. She'd been sitting here beside you for virtually twenty-four hours. But he insisted. With her pregnancy at such a very early stage it's important that she doesn't over-stress herself.'

Twenty-four hours. Annie had sat with him for twenty-four hours!

'How long have I been here?' he asked the nurse.

'Mmm…nearly two days. The impact of the car knocked you out, and then Dr Spears had to sedate you so that he could examine you properly. He was concerned that there might be some permanent damage to your back, but luckily for you there isn't. You've been drifting in and out of consciousness all afternoon, but I think you're finally with us this time.'

'I want to go home,' Dominic told her, moving to throw back the covers and climb out of the hospital bed. The nurse laughed.

'What? Wired up to one of our precious machines?'

As Dominic turned his head he realised what she meant, his forehead pleating in a frown as he looked down at the wires attached to his body.

'If I'm all right, what am I doing with all this?' he demanded shortly.

'You're being monitored,' the nurse told him dryly. 'It's what we do in hospitals. Although you probably don't feel it, your body's still in shock,' she told him in a kinder voice. 'Nothing was broken by the impact when the car hit you, but you are very badly bruised and you're going to find it very painful, if not impossible, to move properly for quite a substantial length of time.'

'How long is that?' Dominic asked her suspiciously.

'Well... Ah, here's Dr Spears,' she announced, smiling at the man who had walked into Dominic's room.

'All I want to know is how soon I can go home,' Dominic told the doctor when the nurse had left. 'I want to see my wife; she's pregnant.'

'Yes, I know,' the doctor confirmed, misunderstanding what Dominic had been about to say. 'Poor girl. I don't think she knew which of you to be the more anxious about at first. But once we'd reassured her that baby is tucked away safely, just where he or she ought to be, she was able to concentrate all her anxiety on you. I've sent her home now. She needed some rest.'

'She shouldn't be on her own,' Dominic told him fiercely. 'She suffered a bad accident herself some years ago and...'

'Yes, I do know,' the doctor told him gently. 'I was on duty when they brought her in. But I think you'll find you're worrying unnecessarily. The maternal instinct is very strong and it empowers a woman with a very special kind of strength.'

'I want to go home,' Dominic repeated.

'Not yet,' the doctor told him calmly. 'I want to see that bruising come down a little bit more first. Ah, good, here's Nurse with a painkilling injection for you.'

'I don't want...' Dominic began, but it was too late, the nurse was already skilfully inserting the hypodermic into his skin and within seconds he could feel himself starting to drift towards unconsciousness.

CHAPTER TEN

'DOMINIC will be able to come home today.'

'Yes, I know,' said Annie as she put down the cup of coffee Helena had just made her. 'They rang me from the hospital earlier. I'm going to pick him up this afternoon and—'

'When are you going to tell him about the baby?' Helena interrupted her to ask.

Immediately Annie looked away from her, her voice tense as she told her, 'I'm not.' She defended her decision when Helena didn't answer. 'There isn't any point. I've told you what happened before, what I remembered. Nothing's changed, Helena.'

'No, nothing's changed,' Helena agreed. 'You *still* love him. You've admitted that.'

'Yes. Yes, I do. But this baby...' She touched her stomach tenderly. 'This baby...*my* baby, has to come first, Helena.'

'The hospital are only releasing Dominic because they think you're going to be on hand to look after him. He's still very badly bruised.'

'Yes, I know,' Annie agreed. 'And I shall be. The baby doesn't show,' she told her quickly. 'It's not... I'm not... I owe him that much, Helena. After all, if he hadn't done what he did...'

'You don't have to justify your decision to me,' Helena told her dryly. 'Although I wouldn't be your

163

friend if I didn't counsel you to think again. This child is *his* child as well as yours, you know.'

'No, it's mine,' Annie insisted fiercely. '*He* won't want it; I know that already. I can remember how it was before.'

'That was five years ago,' Helena reminded her.

'Five years—fifty years. A leopard doesn't change its spots,' Annie returned grimly.

'No,' Helena agreed. 'But a man isn't a leopard and he *can* change his *mind*.'

'A man can,' Annie allowed. 'But *I* don't intend to change *mine*.'

It was nearly a week now since the accident, and every day she had gone to the hospital to see Dominic, remembering how important contact with the outside world had been for her.

He was on his feet now, and walking, despite the pain she knew he had to be suffering from his bruises.

There was still a dressing on his leg, where the flesh had been scraped raw, which had to be changed every day.

'Will you be able to cope?' the doctor had asked her the previous day.

But before she had been able to reply Dominic had announced sharply, 'She won't have to. I can do it myself.'

'Yes, I can cope,' Annie had answered him quietly, ignoring Dominic.

Now, with her pregnancy properly confirmed, there were things she had to do, plans she had to make. But they would have to be put on hold until Dominic was fully back on his feet—she owed him that.

'Lean on me,' she instructed him now, as he hobbled towards the door to his room. 'The car isn't very far away, but if you'd like a wheelchair…'

'What I'd like,' Dominic told her grittily, 'is to be treated like the adult I am and *not* a child. I *can* walk, Annie.'

Only the memory of how she herself had felt whilst she was recuperating enabled Annie to bite back the sharp words hovering on her tongue.

He looked surprisingly fit for a man who had been in hospital for close on a week. His skin was still tanned, his body still full of that sensual male power that made her own tighten and shiver slightly.

As he forced himself not to give in to the pain of his bruises Dominic wondered when Annie was going to tell him about the baby. Not once during her visits had she made *any* reference to it, and he was angrily aware of how inappropriate their current role reversal was. He was the one who should be taking care of *her*, cherishing her, guarding her, protecting her.

'Dr Spears said it might be more comfortable for you to sleep downstairs for the time being,' Annie announced once they were in the car—Dominic's car, not her own, because the seats were more comfortable and there was more leg room for him, even if she herself would have preferred to have been driving her own car.

'No way! For God's sake, I'm *not* an invalid!'

Dominic exploded angrily. 'I don't *need* molly-coddling Annie. In fact...'

'In fact what?' she challenged him sharply. 'In fact you'd prefer me to leave? There's no way that the hospital would have let you come home if they thought you were going to be on your own,' she reminded him.

Want her to *leave*! Dominic looked out of the car window. When they had told him how she had insisted on staying at his bedside until she knew he was going to make a full recovery he had thought...hoped... But in the days since he had recovered consciousness, instead of drawing closer together, instead of him having an opportunity to tell her how thrilled he was about the baby and how much he wanted them to put the past behind them and start again, Annie seemed to have thrown up a wall between them which she had no intention of allowing him to cross.

'We're here,' she announced unnecessarily as she turned into the drive and parked the car. 'You stay here. I'll go and unlock the door and then I'll come back for you.'

Dominic let her get as far as the front door before he opened his own car door and struggled out.

Standing on the gravel of the drive was, for some reason, much harder and much more painful than standing beside his hospital bed—and as for walking...! Gritting his teeth, he started to move towards the house.

Annie finally realised what he was doing when she

had unlocked the door and turned back towards the
car.

'Dominic!' she protested sharply, hurrying towards him and reaching him just as he sagged
heavily to one side, breathing hard.

'I'm all right. For God's sake, stop fussing,' he
told her curtly.

'You're *not* all right. You should have waited for
me.'

'Waited for you?'

She watched his mouth twisting bitterly.

'What good would that do me, Annie? What good
has it ever done me?'

If she didn't know better she might have thought
that there was more than just physical pain she could
see in his eyes. But what was the point in tormenting
herself? Dominic had told her himself that he no
longer loved her.

With only herself to consider she might have been
tempted into the weakness of allowing the physical
desire she could sense he still felt for her to have free
rein, but the knowledge that soon she would have
another, much more vulnerable life to consider had
given her a strength she hadn't known she could pos-
sess. No matter how much her body might ache for
him she could never now accept the shallow worth-
lessness of mere sexual satisfaction.

'Dr Spears gave me some painkillers for you,' she
said calmly. 'Once you're in bed I'll bring you
some.'

They were inside the house now, and as she looked
at the stairs, and then at him, she told him, 'I've got

to go back to the car for your bag, and then I'll help you upstairs.'

'No,' he told her swiftly. 'I *can* manage. If I lean on you it could hurt you.'

Hurt her? He was concerned about *hurting* her... *Now*! After what he had already done... Annie didn't know whether to laugh or cry, but he did have a point. If he should fall...

Helplessly she watched as he struggled painfully up the stairs. When he reached the top he leaned heavily on the balustrade. Anxiously she rushed towards him. She could see the pain etched into his face. Automatically she went to take his arm, ignoring his anger as she helped him into his room.

'Thank you. But I can undress myself,' he gritted. 'Unless, of course, you want to watch!'

Her face burning, Annie fled. She, more than anyone else, understood how pain and incapacity could sharpen even the sweetest temper, but the mere thought of him naked... Pink-cheeked, she hurried back downstairs. The thought of Dominic naked was not a thought she should allow herself to have, she told herself sternly.

It was later that night when a sound from Dominic's room disturbed her own sleep. Automatically she was out of bed, reaching for her robe, pulling it on as she hurried anxiously towards his door.

The anguished groan that reached her ears as she opened the door had her scurrying towards the bed.

Dominic was lying in the middle of it, the bed-clothes pushed down to expose his naked body, the bruises still livid against his tan, the dressing on his leg a paler blur.

Hastily averting her gaze from the very visual evidence of his maleness, Annie leaned across him, intending to reach for the bedclothes to cover him up. But as she did so he suddenly opened his eyes and grasped her arm.

'Annie,' he whispered hoarsely. 'I was just dreaming about you.'

Annie licked her lips a little nervously.

'You're so beautiful,' Dominic told her softly. 'So very, very beautiful.'

His fingers were caressing her arm, making her shiver, making her...

'Dominic, stop it,' she protested. 'You aren't well. You shouldn't...'

'I shouldn't what?' he demanded softly. 'I shouldn't make love to my wife? They said at the hospital that I should do whatever I felt able to do, and I feel very, very able to make love to you, my Annie...*very* able!'

His Annie! She wasn't that now...not any more.

'Dominic,' she whispered in a paper-thin voice. But somehow she was still bending towards him, still allowing him to draw her down beside him to hold her, touch her, kiss her.

'I can remember the first time we made love here,' he was telling her, and Annie had to stop herself from responding. So can I.

She didn't want to tell him she was leaving him until she was sure he was well enough to look after himself. She didn't want to argue or quarrel with him at all, she recognised. Giddily he started to kiss her, and her head began to swim.

'It was so good between us…I wish you could remember,' he was telling her as he reached inside her robe and started to stroke his hand over her body. Was it her imagination or did they linger deliberately on the still flat plane of her tummy?

'I wanted you so much then,' he told her rawly. 'I want you just as much now, Annie.'

It must be the drugs that were making him like this, Annie decided as her breathing quickened and shallowed in response to the desire that he was arousing in her. She could feel her nipples peaking, hardening, aching for much, much more than the delicate brush of his fingertips against them.

'Dominic, no,' she told him as he rolled her gently onto her back and started to kiss her throat, then her breasts.

'Annie, yes,' he whispered back in response as his hands warmed her body.

It was her dreams…her memories…her longings brought vividly to life—and more. She ought to stop him—now—whilst she still could. He wasn't well and she wasn't… But instead of pushing him away she suddenly discovered that she was holding on to him, crying out softly to him…*for* him—too caught up in what she was feeling herself to be shocked by the raw immediacy of his fierce possession of her.

'Is this all right for you?' he asked as he entered her, full and hard, and yet somehow gentle too, as though…

'I want you to…' To stop, she had intended to tell

him, but suddenly her voice was suspended as her need for him overwhelmed her and she was crying out helplessly to him. 'I want you to love me, Dominic. I want you to hold me, fill me...love me—'

Briefly even her baby was forgotten in her desire to absorb and accommodate as much of him as she could, and when she felt him holding back she pressed closer to him, urging him on.

'Yes, oh, yes, that feels so good,' she encouraged him as her fingers tightened against his buttocks and her back arched. 'Oh, yes, Dom... Dom... Yes... Oh... Oh, yes, my darling—yes!'

'Dominic, your leg—your bruises,' Annie gasped in remorse several minutes later, when she had come back down to earth enough to realise what they had done.

'What leg...what bruises?' Dominic teased her.

She could feel the laughter rocking his body just as she had felt the passion moving it only minutes before. What she had done was wrong. Inexcusable. Tears blurred her eyes, but when she moved to pull away from him Dominic held onto her.

'No!' he commanded fiercely, his voice softening as he told her, 'I want you here with me, Annie. I need you here...please stay.'

Please stay! In the darkness Annie fought against her own emotions. He was only being like this because of the drugs he was on, because he felt vulnerable. She waited until she was sure he was asleep before sliding out from beneath his restraining arm and picking up her discarded robe. Her own bed felt cold and lonely…empty. Every time she closed her eyes she could see him…feel him…

Dominic frowned as he watched Annie through his study window. She was outside in the garden, where she had gone to get some mint for the lamb they were having for their meal. He had been home a number of days now, and she had still made no mention to him of her pregnancy. Since the first night he had been home and he had made love with her the atmosphere between them had been distant and strained. He couldn't blame her for *that*. She had every reason to feel angry that he had taken advantage of her kind-heartedness—of her. As he watched her walk slowly, reluctantly, back to the house and him, he made up his mind that if *she* wasn't going to broach the subject of the baby then he would have to do so.

'You aren't eating your lamb,' Annie protested as Dominic pushed away his meal without finishing it.

'No,' he agreed curtly. 'I'm not particularly hungry. Annie, there's something—'

'But lamb always used to be your favourite,' Annie interrupted him anxiously, and then stopped, ashen-faced, as she realised what she had said. She could see the way Dominic was looking at her—the anger in his eyes.

There was a long sharp silence before he demanded, 'You've remembered?'

'Yes,' she was forced to concede.

'When?' Dominic questioned her insistently, repeating the demand with even harsher emphasis when Annie turned her head away before answering him.

'It was…it was before your accident,' she admitted unwillingly, insisting, when he made no response, 'I *would* have told you…I was *going* to tell you, but…'

'But you preferred to keep it to yourself,' Dominic finished angrily for her. 'I wonder why?' he asked sarcastically. 'Or do I? Why *did* you walk out on me, Annie? *Was* it just because of a childish tantrum, or because you realised you didn't really love me?'

'No,' she told him quietly.

'No?' He continued to look at her before repeating harshly, '*No*? Is that it? I want to know everything, Annie.'

The flash of anger in his eyes made her quail a little, but she refused to let him see it.

'Everything? Very well, I shall tell you "everything",' she agreed proudly, her own eyes darkening with her own reciprocal emotions.

Now that it was here—the moment she had been dreading, the confrontation she knew they would have, the final hurdle she had to clear before she could finally draw a line under the part of her life that included him and walk away—the relief she had expected and hoped to feel was lost, submerged beneath the pressure of her other emotions.

It had been a mistake to give in to that wanton need she had had for him the first night he had been home. Making love with him had aroused all manner of needs, feelings—thoughts she simply didn't have the spare capacity to deal with.

'Well?' Dominic pressed through gritted teeth.

He wanted an explanation for why she had left him? Well, he should have one. She took a deep breath, and then, to her own dismay, she heard herself blurting out emotionally, 'I'm leaving you, Dominic. I can't stay here any longer. I don't owe you any explanations. There's no reason…no need for us to be together any more.'

'What?' Dominic demanded harshly, leaning across the table and placing his palms down on it, either side of her. 'I should have thought you and I had an *excellent* reason for being together. The baby,' he elaborated when Annie remained stubbornly silent. '*Our* baby.'

Annie gasped. He *knew*. How? When?

'They told me at the hospital,' he informed her, reading her mind.

'It isn't your baby,' Annie told him stiffly, looking away from him. 'It's mine.' She gave him a tight little smile. 'You see, I *haven't* forgotten.' She took a deep breath. 'I've remembered *exactly* why we quarrelled, Dominic, *and* what you said to me… about…about not wanting me to have your child— about wanting me to abort it.'

'What?' Dominic had gone white. He came round to her side of the table and grasped her upper arms, giving her a grimly emotional little shake as he demanded, 'You were pregnant *then*? You—'

'No,' Annie had to admit. 'No, I wasn't. But I *thought* I might be, and I was afraid. You told me you didn't want me to have your child because of my background, my bad blood. That's why I... I tried to tell you but you wouldn't listen. You...'

'What? I said *no* such thing,' Dominic objected, horrified. 'Annie...'

'You did,' Annie insisted. 'You said you didn't want to burden a child with—'

'With a father who couldn't be there for it. A father who put his career before it, as my parents had done. I know how it feels to grow up realising that you're not totally loved by your parents—*that* was the burden I was referring to, not...'

He stopped, white to the lips, shaking his head as he protested,

'Annie, how *could* you have thought...believed...? I *loved* you. I...I didn't think either of us was emotionally ready to be a good parent, it's true, and perhaps I did overreact... But I never... If I'd thought for one moment you'd believed you were already pregnant... I simply thought you were in danger of succumbing to an impulse—that you wanted a baby because you were afraid of being alone. I never...'

Her revelations had stunned and appalled him. They had hurt him as well, he recognised, but he forced himself to set aside that feeling, to remember Annie as she had been then, to understand and remember how she had felt about her unknown parentage. He took a deep breath. Somehow he had to find a way of reassuring her, convincing her... showing her just how wrong she had been.

'Whoever and whatever your parents were doesn't

matter, Annie. What matters is that *you* are you—a wonderful, special, individual person who logically must carry something of both of them within your genes.'

He reached out and cupped her face before she could move away, his eyes dark with the intensity of his emotions as he told her fiercely, 'You may never have known them, Annie, but I know that I would be as proud to have them as my child's grandparents as I am to have you as its mother. What you are, *all* that you are, shows in everything about you—your honesty, your compassion, your courage, your intelligence, and most of all your love.

'I wish that I could say the same about my own genetic inheritance. My parents were thoughtless, selfish, stubborn, totally wrapped up in their own concerns. I was an encumbrance they didn't really want, a nuisance farmed out into the care of my grandparents, who looked on me as a duty...a responsibility. *That* was the genetic inheritance I didn't want my child to have.'

As she searched his face Annie knew that he was telling her the truth. Tears blurred her vision.

Dominic leaned forward. Sensing that he was about to kiss her, she panicked and pulled away. She needed time to absorb what he had told her, to accept it and to accept that she had misjudged him. That she had left him—destroyed their marriage and their love for nothing. Was there any way she could ever accept the enormity of that?

Silently Dominic let her go. It was symptomatic of everything that had gone wrong between them that even now they couldn't share their feelings—that there were barriers between them.

Love might grow quickly but trust was another matter. Trust was a slow-growing plant that needed nurturing. His fault was that he had not seen and responded to Annie's need for that careful nurturing—and hers... She owned no fault, he recognised. She had simply reacted out of fear to his crass thoughtlessness.

Annie didn't know what hurt most—knowing that the love she and Dominic had once shared was lost to her for ever or knowing that her own lack of self-esteem, her own fear of the unknownness of her background, had led to its destruction. But what was worse, much worse, than her own pain was the pain she was going to inflict on her child, who would now have to grow up without the benefit of the loving closeness of both its parents.

She loved Dominic totally, completely, irreversibly, irretrievably. She knew that now. She knew, too, that he still found her desirable. But desire wasn't love, and he had already told her quite plainly that his reason, his only reason, for wanting her back in his life was so that she could provide him with the answers he needed before he drew a line under their marriage and divorced her.

This morning he had walked downstairs unaided. It was time for her to go whilst she could still go with dignity and with pride.

She packed quietly and efficiently and then went to find him. He was in the kitchen.

'It's time for me to go,' she told him calmly. 'We both know the answer to your question now. The divorce should go through easily enough, and—'

'The divorce? *What* divorce?' Dominic demanded grimly. 'You're carrying my child, Annie. There's no way I'm going to…we can't divorce now.'

Annie's face paled. Deep down inside she had feared he would react like this, but she had told herself she was strong enough to resist the temptation he was offering her.

'Look,' he said, more gently, 'I know we've got some bridge-building to do. I know you need time. Trust isn't something that grows overnight, but I know we can make it work.'

Annie could feel herself start to quake deep down inside with the effort of trying to hold onto reality, trying to remind herself of what reality was, and the fact that he no longer loved her whilst she…

From somewhere she managed to dredge up the necessary will-power.

'I realise you are speaking out of some misguided sense of responsibility and…and duty, Dominic,' she told him. 'But—'

'It wasn't *responsibility* that made me want you in my bed the other night,' Dominic interrupted her trenchantly. 'And, forgive me if I'm being ungallant, I don't think it was *duty* that kept you there either.'

'That's not fair,' Annie gasped in outrage. 'What happened then was…was…'

'Was what?' Dominic encouraged her softly. 'Or shall I tell you what it was?' When she made no answer he continued in a sexy whisper, 'What happened then was what nature designed us to *have* happen, my Annie. What happened then was…'

She tensed as his voice dropped even lower.

'I've *never* stopped loving you and I don't think that you've ever stopped loving me. Consciously you may have forgotten me, pushed me to the back of your mind, but deep down inside you *couldn't* forget… Deep down inside you, your love, like mine, *couldn't* be extinguished. We owe it to the baby to give ourselves…our *love*…another chance, Annie.'

'No.' Immediately she shook her head in denial.

For a moment Dominic was silent, and then, just as she thought he was going to accept her denial of him and turn away, he cupped her face and said, so gently that it made her heart turn over inside her body, 'Do you know what I think? I think that you're afraid to…'

'I'm not afraid of anything,' Annie denied quickly. 'I can manage by myself, Dominic. I don't need…'

'…me?' he finished quietly for her. 'Maybe you don't, Annie. But this…' He touched her tummy gently. 'Our son or our daughter does. We both know what it's like to grow up alone, isolated…feeling different…feeling unloved…'

'My baby *will* be loved,' Annie insisted stiffly. 'I shall love it. You can't make me stay here, Dominic. You can't make me stay married to you.'

As he searched her face she instinctively turned away, trying to hide herself from him. He had been right when he accused her of being afraid—not that she would ever admit it to him. She *was* afraid…very afraid. How could she take the risk of believing him?

'No, I can't make you stay,' he agreed heavily as he released her.

What had she expected? What had she wanted? For him to physically hold onto her?

Without looking at him she edged round the kitchen door and then fled into the hallway, where she had left her things.

'I've never stopped loving you,' he had said. But how *could* she believe him? How could she be sure he wasn't just saying it to protect their child?

The door to Dominic's study stood open. Impulsively she tiptoed inside. The room was empty, the curtains blowing in the breeze. A piece of paper had been blown down onto the floor. Automatically she bent to pick it up, and then froze as she replaced it on the desk. In the half-open drawer she could see a photograph frame. Carefully she picked it up, studying the five-year-old photograph. It was her and Dominic on their wedding day. She remembered how Dominic had insisted that they had the photo taken. Tears filled her eyes, her fingertips trembling as she pressed them against the cool glass.

She had been so happy that day, so filled with joy and love. Dominic had, in truth, been her perfect lover, her dream hero...her love... But he was five years older now, and a different person. They were both different people. Different outwardly, perhaps, but inside, their emotions...their love...

She could feel the pain turning and twisting inside her. But if she gave in to Dominic now how would she ever know if he really wanted her?

Quickly she replaced the photograph, and then

closed the window before walking back into the hall-way and picking up her bags.

Her keys in one hand and her bags in the other, she opened the front door and looked towards her car.

Dominic! What on earth...? She swallowed hard, and then blinked. Dominic was standing beside her car, a heavy bag at his feet.

'If you won't live with me, my Annie, then I'm just going to have to live with you,' Dominic told her simply. 'Where you go—I go. There isn't any way there's going to be another disappearing act.'

'You can't do this,' Annie protested thickly. 'You don't want me...it's just because of the baby...'

'Really? Is that what you think?' Dominic asked her politely, so politely and so calmly that Annie was taken off guard. He dropped his case and came strid-ing towards her, saying softly, 'Well, I'll just have to prove to you how wrong you are, won't I?'

She had left it too late to turn and run. 'Dominic,' she protested. 'No. You mustn't...your leg...' But the remainder of her denial was lost against the soft-ness of his shirt as he swept her up into his arms and strode through the house with her and up the stairs.

'It was in this room, this bed, that we made love as only lovers can,' he whispered softly to her as he laid her on it. 'This bed where I *showed* you just how much I love you Annie. It was here, too, that you showed me your love—told me of it.'

'That was five years ago,' she protested sharply. 'And...'

'No. I don't mean *then*,' Dominic denied, smiling

dangerously at her as he reminded her, 'Our child was conceived in this bed…the night you told me I was your dream lover come true, the night you told me how much—'

'No!' Annie protested weakly, covering her ears, her face hot with self-consciousness.

'Yes,' Dominic insisted thickly as he took advantage of her occupied hands to cup her face and look down into her eyes. 'Both of us have unhappy memories…fears and doubts. But what we really feel for one another… Give yourself to me now,' he whispered to her, 'and then tell me if you dare that you don't love me…that you don't feel my love for you, that you and I don't have a future together.'

'Please don't do this,' Annie begged painfully. 'I don't want…'

'You don't want what?' Dominic asked her gently. 'You don't want this?'

She moaned beneath her breath as he kissed her and her resistance started to melt. She could feel the heat of her own desire licking through her veins, her flesh.

'You don't want me?' Dominic pressed as his tongue twined with hers and her body arched tautly against him. 'Or this…?'

He was nibbling at the vulnerable column of her throat, his hands stroking at her skin—her bare skin, Annie realised fatalistically as he skilfully swept away her clothes along with her inhibitions.

'You're a magician…a warlock…' she told him resentfully, her voice as clouded with her emotions as her eyes, her body already heavily languorous with her love and longing.

'I'm a man,' Dominic corrected, adding possessively, 'And you're my woman, my Annie. My love, my only love...'

She heard him groan as she felt the hot satin of his bare body against her own, felt him shudder as his need convulsed him.

'I love you so much,' he told her. 'Please, please love me in return. You're my life, my love...my past, my present and my future, Annie. Without you...'

His mouth brushed her nipples, taut and tender now with her desire for him, and she cried out, unable to resist the temptation to move closer to him, to wrap her arms around him and hold him captive against her body...within her body... She felt the ecstatic ripple of pleasure flow through her as he entered her, so gently, and she knew he was deliberately holding himself back because of the baby... their baby...

When she started to cry he licked away her tears, holding her, comforting her, telling her that she was crying away her pain, and suddenly she knew that it was true. She could almost feel the tide of her emotions turning, the happiness and the love flowing back through her body. Dream lovers were all very well in their way, but *this* was reality, and the reality was...the reality was...

'Mmm?' Dominic encouraged as he realised she was trying to speak.

'I love you,' Annie sighed mundanely, but to Dominic the simple words were as powerful as the most passionate love prose that had ever been written.

EPILOGUE

'WHAT'S the A for?' Helena asked curiously as she watched Annie inscribing the invitations to her six-month-old daughter's christening.

'Amnesia,' Dominic replied for her with a teasing grin. 'So that we can both remember how she came into being.'

'Oh, no,' Helena protested. 'Surely you aren't…?' She stopped as she saw the laughing shake of her head that Annie was giving her husband.

Helena and Bob had called round to see them to discuss the arrangements for the christening.

'We ought to ring them first,' Bob had warned her. 'You know what happened the last time we called unexpectedly. We quite obviously interrupted them in the middle of making love.'

'Yes, but that was four months ago, when Charlotte was eight weeks old and Annie had been given the all-clear by her gynaecologist.'

'I don't care. You only have to see those two to know that it's damn near impossible for them to keep their hands off one another,' Bob told her forthrightly.

'Well, they've got five missing years to catch up on,' Helena had reminded him.

She had never seen a couple so much in love with one another. Annie was practically incandescent with

it, and as for Dominic… She wasn't sure when she
had seen him looking more proud—the day he and
Annie had renewed their vows to one another, a
month before Charlotte's birth, or the first time he
had actually held his newborn daughter.

'The A is for Alice,' Annie told Helena, giving
Dominic a stern look.

'Alice. Oh, that's my middle name.' Helena
beamed.

'Yes, I know,' Annie told her lovingly, getting up
to go and give her friend a hug as she saw the way
Helena's face pinkened with colour and her eyes
sheened over with tears.

'I'm too *old* to be her godmother,' she had protested when Annie had told her of their plans, but
Annie and Dominic had overcome all her objections,
and the truth was that she was thrilled at the thought
of having her as her godchild.

'Charlotte Alice sounds lovely,' she approved,
when she had her emotions back under control.

'Charlotte Amnesia sounds better,' Dominic argued. 'And we'd never forget it…'

'Ignore him,' Annie told her friend, picking up a
cushion, which she threw at her husband.

As he caught it Helena heard him whispering to
Annie, 'I'll make you pay for that…later!'

It was growing dark when Helena and Bob left, and
as she turned in her seat to reach for her seat belt,
as Bob drove down the drive Helena saw an upstairs
bedroom light go on in the house behind them. She

knew it was the light to Annie and Dominic's bedroom.

'For heaven's sake, Dominic,' Annie scolded her
husband as he bundled her onto the bed.

'You're wearing far too many clothes—do you
know that?' he whispered, mock naughtily.

'Helena and Bob will have seen the light go on,
and they'll know...'

'They'll know what?' he asked her softly. 'That I
can't wait to make love to my wife?' He laughed as
he saw the way Annie was blushing. 'Besides,' he
teased her. 'Wasn't it *you* who said just before they
went that you fancied an early night?'

'An early *night*,' Annie agreed. 'Not— Oh...' She
gave a small gasp as Dominic touched her, and then
another, before protesting longingly, 'Dominic...'

'Mmm...?' he encouraged.

'It doesn't matter,' Annie breathed as her arms
opened to wrap round him. 'Nothing matters. Only
you...only... Mmm...'

'Mmm...' he agreed sexily as he nuzzled her skin.

'Amnesia...' Annie breathed raggedly. 'Poor
Helena. You shouldn't tease her...you shouldn't...'

Her voice faded away into a soft sigh of female
pleasure as his touch grew bolder and more intimate
and her body responded to him.

In the cot in the nursery the little girl, whose parents'
private secret name for her was always going to be
Amnesia, smiled contentedly up at the mobile danc-
ing over her head.

*   *   *

'No wonder I could never truly forget you,' Annie sighed sensuously.

'Your dream lover,' Dominic told her.

'The reality is far, far better than my dreams,' Annie assured him lovingly. 'The reality...*my* reality...is you, Dominic...you and Charlotte Alice and our lives together, our future together... The reality is—oh, Dominic!'

*An electric chemistry with a disturbingly
familiar stranger...
A reawakening of passions long forgotten...
And a compulsive desire to get to know
this stranger all over again!*

Because

**What the memory has lost,
the body never forgets**

In Harlequin Presents®
over the coming months look out for:

BACK IN THE MARRIAGE BED
by Penny Jordan
On sale September, #2129

SECRET SEDUCTION
by Susan Napier
On sale October, #2135

THE SICILIAN'S MISTRESS
by Lynne Graham
On sale November, #2139

Available wherever Harlequin books are sold.

HARLEQUIN®
Makes any time special ™

Visit us at www.eHarlequin.com   HPAMN

Coming this September from

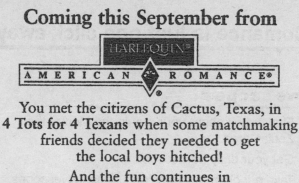

HARLEQUIN®

A M E R I C A N ◆ R O M A N C E®

You met the citizens of Cactus, Texas, in
4 Tots for 4 Texans when some matchmaking
friends decided they needed to get
the local boys hitched!

And the fun continues in

3 TOTS
BY
JUDY
CHRISTENBERRY
for TEXANS

Don't miss...

THE $10,000,000 TEXAS WEDDING

September 2000
HAR #842

In order to claim his $10,000,000 inheritance,
Gabe Dawson had to find a groom for Katherine Peters
or else walk her down the aisle himself. But when he
tried to find the perfect man for the job, the list of
candidates narrowed down to one man—*him!*

Available at your favorite retail outlet.

HARLEQUIN®
Makes any time special ™

Visit us at www.eHarlequin.com

HARTOS2

Romance is just one click away!

love scopes

➤ Find out all about your guy in the Men of the Zodiac area.

➤ Get your daily horoscope.

➤ Take a look at our Passionscopes, Lovescopes, Birthday Scopes and more!

join Heart-to-Heart, our interactive community

➤ Talk with Harlequin authors!

➤ Meet other readers and chat with other members.

➤ Join the discussion forums and post messages on our message boards.

romantic ideas

➤ Get scrumptious meal ideas in the Romantic Recipes area!

➤ Check out the Daily Love Dose to get romantic ideas and suggestions.

Visit us online at

www.eHarlequin.com

on Women.com Networks

HEUT2

**Don't miss
an exciting opportunity
to save on the purchase of
Harlequin and Silhouette books!**

Buy any two Harlequin or
Silhouette books and save
$10.00 off future Harlequin
and Silhouette purchases

OR

buy any three
Harlequin or Silhouette books
and save **$20.00 off** future
Harlequin and Silhouette purchases.

**Watch for details
coming in October 2000!**

PHQ400

HARLEQUIN®
Makes any time special ™

Silhouette®
Where love comes alive™

Coming Next Month

HARLEQUIN *Presents*

THE BEST HAS JUST GOTTEN BETTER!

#2133 INNOCENT SINS Anne Mather
Eight years ago Laura Neill had innocently stolen into her stepbrother Oliver's room and discovered ecstasy in his arms. This is Laura's first visit home since. Can she face Oliver without confessing the love she still feels for him?

#2134 THE PLAYBOY'S VIRGIN Miranda Lee
Brilliant advertising tycoon Harry Wilde needed a challenge. It came in the guise of Tanya, who'd recently inherited an ailing firm. In no time at all Harry had helped her take charge—and had fallen for her. But Tanya wasn't the marrying kind—and he only ever had affairs....

#2135 SECRET SEDUCTION Susan Napier
Nina had lost her memory, but it was clear that stranger Ryan Flint recognized her. He seemed angry with Nina, and yet intent on seducing her. When their passion finally exploded, what secrets would be revealed?

#2136 MISTRESS OF THE SHEIKH Sandra Marton
Sheikh Nicholas al Rashid is hailed in his homeland as the Lion of the Desert, and Amanda has been commissioned to refurbish his already luxurious Manhattan apartment. Just why does Nick seem so intent on making Amanda his mistress?

#2137 A MOST PASSIONATE REVENGE Jacqueline Baird
When Rose meets society bachelor Xavier Valdespino again, he immediately whisks her to Spain and blackmails her into marriage. But despite their steamy love life, Rose soon discovers Xavier's true motivation: revenge!

#2138 THE BABY BOND Sharon Kendrick
Normally Angelica would have liked nothing better than to look after Rory's orphaned nephew—she adored babies. But this baby was her ex-husband's love child, and Rory was the brother-in-law who'd always held an illicit attraction for her....

CNM0900